H. R Haweis

Ideals for Girls

H. R Haweis

Ideals for Girls

ISBN/EAN: 9783337065850

Printed in Europe, USA, Canada, Australia, Japan

Cover: Foto ©Andreas Hilbeck / pixelio.de

More available books at **www.hansebooks.com**

IDEALS FOR GIRLS ❧ BY THE REV. H. R. HAWEIS M.A. ❧ AUTHOR OF MUSIC AND MORALS ❧ ❧ ❧ ❧ ❧

LONDON: JAMES BOWDEN
10 HENRIETTA STREET, W.C.
NEW YORK: M. F. MANSFIELD
22 EAST SIXTEENTH STREET, 1897

CONTENTS

IDEALS

Untidy
Girls

UNTIDY GIRLS

OH, well,' you say, 'some people are *naturally* neat and tidy, and others are not;' and if you don't happen to be tidy yourself, you fancy you have disposed of the question by that word *naturally*, as who should say, 'No one should be required to be *un*naturally tidy!' But in your case, my dear young lady, that is just the point. No one asks you 'to affect a virtue if you have it not,' but to *acquire* what you have not got if it is good—in short, to *become*, not to *pretend to be* what you are not. The whole duty of man—ay, and woman too—consists in becoming what you are not by nature, and in acquiring what you were not born with. Why, that is the secret of discipline, and it makes all the difference between you and a savage. Now, if you notice that others are tidy naturally, whilst it is a strain and burden upon you even to

put away your work or see that it is put away,
console yourself by reflecting that Anna, who is
always neat and orderly by a sort of instinct,
would give anything for your voice. Well, it
is not necessary that a girl should be able to
sing, but it is very necessary that she should
be tidy. A beautiful voice is a gift, but order
is a grace as well as a gift, and the difference
between them is this, that a grace may be won
by you, whilst a gift is yours by nature, and you
cannot win it.

Now, Anna sings like a peacock, and she has a
bad ear for music, but she is a model of neatness
and order ; whilst you warble like a nightingale,
but 'you can never find anything'—simply because you never put anything away ; and as for
your dress—'sloven' is not the word !

So far the little moral (if any moral is little)
stands, 'Let those who have gifts cultivate
graces of their own, and let those who have won
graces not despise the gifts others are born with.'
For let me add that as human nature is made, it
is very common to find people esteeming lightly
or even sneering at qualities which they do not
happen to possess. For instance, singing Jenny
will say of neat Anna, 'Prim, stuck-up little
thing ! with her pincushion in one pocket and

her thimble in another, and her ridiculous chatelaine, with scissors, tablet, a looking-glass, sticking-plaster, and bodkins!' And I am sorry to say that prim Anna is apt to say of singing Jenny, 'Oh, Jenny—she thinks of nothing but showing off—to see her flirting and making eyes over the piano at the men! A little music is all very well, but to be always humming about the house, and singing those ridiculous love songs after dinner, I have no patience with her! I really do wonder she is not a little ashamed of herself, after all,' etc. etc.

Now, Jenny, it is with you, and not with prim Anna, that I want to have a word to-day. No one doubts that you can sing, but every one sees that you are a sloven born, and I who have observed you, and like you very much, and admire your singing, and think you have many amiable qualities, am quite sure that, as you are very quick and intelligent, if you only had a little more principle—yes, my dear, *principle* is what you want—you could mend your glaring defects ; for disorder, be you well assured, is a moral defect, and if you would take a little trouble you could be as charming again, and two or three times more useful and perhaps even more happy than you are now.

'But what am I to do?' says Jenny. 'I know mother is always "going on" at me about my books and drawing things and clothes, and was quite angry with me because she found some hard-boiled eggs which we brought back from the picnic amongst my pocket-handkerchiefs and collars in the wardrobe. But what does it matter? I'm sure I get quite hungry in the night sometimes when I can't sleep, and a hard-boiled egg is such a comfort!'

'Now, Jenny,' I feel inclined to say, 'you have opened the whole question with your "hard-boiled eggs" and "what does it matter?"'

Consider the only thing which really matters in this world is what is right and what is wrong. Amongst other reasons, because peace and happiness, and not unfrequently health or disease, life or death, is at stake.

Now, *order* is right, and *disorder* is wrong ; therefore, to be untidy, slovenly, 'disorderly,' even in a small way, is to be to that extent *immoral*. But people are often slow to grasp a principle until it is enforced by a penalty.

Think, then, Jenny, of the inconvenient waste of your own time, other people's time, and of the confusion, mischief, and injury which you inflict wholesale annually, and in an ever-increasing *ratio*, simply because you 'can't see the harm' of mislaying your things, forgetting your engagements, and keeping hard-boiled eggs in your wardrobe.

'A Time for Everything, and Everything at the Right Time.

'A Place for Everything, and Everything in its Place.'

You should write these two sentences up like texts in big letters—say just above your washhand stand—and they should stare you in the face every morning.

But you are in the habit of reading a novel whilst you dress, and you brush out and do up your hair in between the paragraphs; that accounts for your chignon never being quite straight and your fringe usually in disorder. I have even seen your nails not quite— And that hook in front has been for two days hanging by a thread, so a bit of white lining shows just in front. You came down to breakfast with a black on your nose; the fact is, you had used your curling irons carelessly, and had hardly looked in the glass—it happened to be just at the end of an exciting chapter.

Do one thing at a time, Jenny : *dress*, when you dress ; and when you read, *read*.

Why is your mother left to discover white strings hanging out, buttons off, hair awry ?— whilst over and over again you have scrambled so hastily into your clothes that everything looks as if it had been pitchforked on to your body like a superfluous appendage, or at best, an after-thought !

Then your clothes never ' last '—sometimes bundled into a cupboard when they ought to be shaken out or hung up—or ' nice things ' squashed in drawers — muslin rumpled — silk creased—and the steels or bones in bodices bent or snapped—and you don't like to be lectured ? No, of course not—but why not ? Because you know you deserve it.

But, dear Jenny, you are just seventeen, and you are forming habits which are to be your lifelong plagues or blessings. Do think of the waste, the loss that you inflict on others as well as upon yourself, simply because nothing is ever in its place, and you never know where to lay your hands on what you want, or what other people want. You have got a hole in your pocket—your purse is a small one—if you could lay your hands upon your thimble and a needle

and thread in a moment, you could mend it—
but you can't. Your mother called your attention
to that hole this morning, but you insisted on
wearing that dress, because you said it was a cool
one, and you were in too great a hurry to mend
it. Eleven o'clock comes — by mere chance
you recollect an appointment—you think of that
hole, it is true, but you can't find your thimble,
or your needle and thread—you go all over the
house to get some one to sew up your pocket—
the servant is too busy, your sister is having a
singing lesson—another 'bear hunt' for your
thimble—no good. You've got to catch a train
—bother the pocket!—you'll risk it—and off
you start. Your purse drops out, and is lost ;
it contained a postal order belonging to some
one else—you had to refund the note—half your
month's allowance went too. Your father refused
to refund that, so you could not give that half-
crown you promised to old rheumatic Mrs B., or
the tobacco to old Jones, nor could you buy the
Christmas presents other people had set their
hearts upon, and so forth—all because you did
not mind going about with a hole in your pocket,
which you couldn't mend because you had mis-
laid your ' things.'

You have a bookshelf, but you never put any

books back. Your spelling is not strong—you
are on the point of getting a little engagement—
just two hours in the morning—to teach a
neighbour's child reading and writing. It
would have been a nice addition to your pocket-
money, but in answering the letter you spell
' receive '—' recieve.' The fact is, you would
have looked it out in your dictionary, but you
had not replaced it ; subsequently it was found
amongst your boots in a cupboard—how it got
there no one knows. As usual, you risk the
spelling—and lose your engagement. ' My dear,'
says the lady to a friend,—who, of course, repeats
the observation to you,—' if Miss Jenny can't
spell " receive," she is not fit to teach Dolly.'

You can't find your umbrella,—subsequently it
is discovered lying on the piano—it being wet,
it spoiled the varnish,—you go out without it,
and spoil your new hat.

You forget an engagement to play some one's
accompaniment, or you are an hour late for a
rehearsal, and every one is inconvenienced—next
time you are quietly dropped out of the enter-
tainment, because you can't be depended upon.

You forgot to feed your birds for two days—
you can think of nothing but the new ' bike.'
One is dead.

Your mother trusted you to get a prescription made up ; you thought you put it amongst some papers, but you can't find it—you never will find it, because it is mixed up with a crumpled pocket-handkerchief that has gone to the wash.

Thus, owing to a slipshod, careless, unmethodical, scatter-brain state of mind, you go through life, wasting your own time and inflicting endless annoyances and even injuries on other people. Your mental slovenliness inevitably reflects itself, as I have pointed out, in your personal appearance, and it handicaps you terribly. You are good-natured, and quick and ready enough with repartee ; but the grease spot on your bonnet ribbon has been there for a week—two buttons are off your gloves, and one is off your left boot —there is a little tear just above the fringe of your skirt—and as to the lining of your dress—! Jenny, women's eyes are quick, but men's eyes are critical. To many a man little danger-signals like a grease spot, or (dare I say) a smile disclosing two side-teeth not quite clean, or an unstitched glove, or a hook without an eye, or an eye without a hook—my dear, the results are positively fatal ; for men are not all fools even when they are in love, and they know that a

sloven before marriage is a sloven after marriage—
and men don't like slovens.

I am not for a moment supposing, Jenny, that
you are one of those silly girls who think of
nothing but marriage from the moment they are
in their teens, although I would not, were I you,
affect to despise men, and say, 'I don't mean to
marry.' Wait till you are asked, my dear.

But, married or unmarried, your ruling defect,
in the interest of your friends and of all households you may enter, calls for immediate and
earnest attention. I am sure—because, as you
are a sensible, very well-meaning, and also quite
a pretty and attractive girl—I am sure, Jenny,
you will not leave off reading this paper without
glancing at a few practical rules that will not be
difficult for you to remember, but conformity to
which will be a great help to you, as well as an
inestimable blessing to all those who may have
the privilege of your acquaintance.

First, leave off reading books, writing your
diary, composing verses, or muddling about with
flowers and knick-knacks whilst you are dressing
in the morning. Give your whole mind to the
details of your toilet ; you will dress in half the
time, you will begin the day well, and come
down looking spick and span.

Secondly, keep a little ivory tablet (like prim Anna), and write down your day's engagements, and on your dressing-table or writing-table keep a diary almanac registering your engagements—a month in advance, if needful. Study it carefully every Monday morning so as to see a week ahead, and *every* morning before you go down glance at it for the day's work, and enter from your day tablet any new *mems.* for the following day.

Thirdly, *every Monday* (1) see that all books not in use are put back on your bookshelf—if you labelled and numbered all your books, and always put them in the same order, you would find it save much time and trouble.

(2.) Look into your chests of drawers and cupboards, and see that everything is not in 'a hopeless muddle.' Remember the servant wants looking after; if she sees you don't care, she 'won't bother' about anything.

(3.) See that all ribbons, frocks, boots, gloves, frills, etc., that you expect to wear during the week are clean and mended.

(4.) Arrange your desk and writing-table; keep your bills, letters, and literary papers, if you have got any, separate; and always have on your table indiarubber rings, pins, pencils, and post-cards.

Fourthly, feed your animals regularly every day at fixed times, and see that their cages, kennels, or hutches are properly cleaned.

Fifthly, never undertake in a moment of impulse things you do not seriously intend to do, such as visiting the poor, teaching in Sunday school, training a choir, arranging flowers, superintending the poultry-yard, collecting and figuring the eggs, decorating the dinner-table, or putting down the things for the wash, etc. Better not promise than fail or forget household duties affecting the convenience and comfort of so many people.

And lastly, my dear Jenny, remember that disorder is an *immoral* thing, that a disorderly life is a *sinful* life, that it is your temptation —and having done your best to master such obvious remedies as I have indicated, never rise from your knees in the morning without praying for a quick mind and a ready heart and be sure that spiritual ministries will be attracted to you and 'compass you round about,' so you shall be daily 'on your way attended,' and things will 'be brought to your remembrance,' and you shall have an inclination, even a passion, given you 'both to will and to do His good pleasure' (Phil. ii. 13).

Musical
Girls

MUSICAL
GIRLS

'But are you really musical?

'Oh, I learnt music when I was at school.'

'And a very good thing, too; every one ought to learn music—even if they are not musical. You've got to be trained somehow, and the process of learning your notes when a child, sitting still, correlating sight and touch and observation, all this is brain training, which can be afterwards transferred to any occupation or pursuit, and music in its initial stages is as good as anything else for this, but—are you musical? that was my question. Is sound to you what colour is to a painter, what scent is to an animal, what touch is to the blind? Is it an instinct, a rapture, a magic world of itself?'

'Oh, dear no,' says Constance. 'I don't really care for music; I quite disliked it at school—practising made my fingers ache, and my singing mistress used to worry so about my singing out of tune that I almost dreaded opening my mouth.'

Now, it is quite clear that Constance is not musical. Musical children sing in the cradle; later on, they are always humming or whistling about the house, and fly at a piano or any music-making thing as ducks fly at the water. Of course, there are all degrees. You can have a first, second, or third class musical faculty. The cultivation of second and third class faculties is the bane of the musical world. I should never recommend the manufacture of musicians out of anything but first-class faculty. It is all very well for girls if only of third-class endowment to learn enough of piano to play a dance or accompany a hymn tune—it is good, just as the knowledge of a little cooking or dressmaking is good, it adds to a girl's social utility; but it is never worth while spending much time, money, and trouble upon trying to do what you will never do well—providing you can do something better.

And here a word in the ear of parents. They like their daughters to be 'accomplished,' and 'music and painting' are parts of the 'shibboleth' of a polite education   The daughters may protest; the teachers, if honest, shrug their shoulders, and sometimes retire from an unequal contest with incapacity; but sometimes a fortune is spent, precious time is wasted, and hopeless mediocrity is the result. What is worse still is that the demand of native incompetence has created a *spécialité* similar to our cram coaches for the dull. There are teachers well known for their skill in dealing with musical dolts. They pride themselves on being able to make people play and sing a little who ought never to play and sing at all.

To the young girl I say, find out what you were meant to do, and aim at it. If you make up your mind about it, no sensible parent will continue to waste your time and temper and their own money upon your music—that is, if you are very second or even third rate; nor ought you to be misled by any silly and ill-advised ambition to rival or outshine Fanny, who sings like an angel, or Gerty, who is a pianiste born, '*artiste jusqu'au bouts des doigts.*' In these days, when there are thousands of nice girls who are lost in the crowd of our surplus female population,—hardly 'getting a chance,'—anything which makes a girl stand out and shine, as it were, against a background, anything distinctive which draws attention to her individually, gives her a distinct social advantage. This is the explanation of all dress peculiarity, the wearing of bright colours, flowers, jewels—the passion for the stage—the rage for a vocation—skill in horsemanship or shooting or palmistry, or anything, in short, which makes a girl agreeably or usefully or even oddly exceptional, and picks her out of the crowd ; and the easiest way of accomplishing this is, undoubtedly, to stand up and sing, or better still, play the violin.

Better? I had better have said *worse*. The violin mania has reached proportions which call for a protest. I have always said a beautiful woman, with musical sensibility, playing a beautiful violin as some women can play it, is one of the most beautiful things in the world. But you, my dear Constance, will never play the violin. You only began it at fifteen (that is too old), and then not because you had a good arm or a suitable hand, or were particularly musical, but because you had a pretty face and nice floss-silky yellow hair. That is of no use for playing. Why immolate the violin to your hair ? It makes a musician wild to hear you ; he even gets to hate your hair, and associates the rose bloom of your cheek and your blue eyes with discordant noises. Your fingers are the worst part of you. You haven't got a sinewy or lithe or even a plump hand with taper fingers— no, nor a rounded arm, and you saw round your shoulder ; your red, bony elbows stick out, your fingers are stiff, you can't play your passages, and you scrape horribly. No, Constance, you have no faculty for the violin. You might do better on the piano, but you can't bear practising till your fingers ache, which is absolutely the one thing needful for *technique*. But the violin ! oh ! it is the most exacting of all instruments. You want a special instinct for it. You must woo it *very young*. It must be positively your first and properly your only musical love. But the fact is, as I have so often had occasion to state, we are not a musical people. We are polite to ladies, but not musical. We will not slight a lady *en evidence*, and so if she gets up and poses with the violin so that all are forced to notice her, or if she brings her close personality to bear upon us through her voice, we attend, we listen, though she sings like a peacock or scrapes abominably. But she may play divinely on the piano and no one will listen, because as she sits at the piano she is *efface* and not much *en evidence*.

The enforced attention a violin girl or a singing girl receives conceals from her that she is a nuisance. She creates attention, that is enough—yea, verily, and often too much.

But Ethel, unlike Constance, is not only pretty, but a musical sensitive—music shakes and thrills her nervous system as the wind smites upon an Æolian harp. She feels spiritual analogies in sound, and things she can utter only through sound. She dreams in spheres unknown to those who have not within them the secret of sound, which is so close akin to soul vibrations. The violin beckons her away to enchanted caves, where deep waters seem ever welling in with mysterious murmurs. The violin answers her soul—which no man or woman has ever yet answered ; it vibrates to a hidden pain, wails with her passion and laughs with her exuberant joy. You have played with this mystic friend the violin, Ethel, almost from the nursery. Your hand has grown lovingly about its smooth, shiny neck as you grew into budding womanhood. Your lithe fingers know so well how to caress its vibrating strings and draw forth a sweetness it seems to give to you alone, and all to yourself ; and your bow is as a magic wand where-with you become the gentle but irresistible ruler of the spirits. Let no one persuade you that the piano is better, or beguile you into singing fairly —you who may play the violin supremely well. You are exactly fitted for each other, you and your violin—let well alone. Your hand is happy, and always looks well on the finger-board ; your fingers are flexible ; and your sense of touch at the tips, by use and cultivation, has actually increased just there that mystic nerve fluid which physiologists tell us is actually the same as the thinking grey matter of the brain. This throws a new light on the mystery of touch, of which violin-playing is so perfect an example. Your touch *is* thought. The tips of your fingers *think*. This is quite a new physiological discovery, but it may explain the strange emotions and suggestions conveyed through the thrilling vibration medium of a finger and a violin string. Upon that sound is travelling not only vibrations of feeling, but peradventure vibrations of thought ; for once in the subtle realm of molecular and ethereal vibration-waves, and who shall tell by what subtle alchemy physical vibration is converted into the mental brain-wave which is thought ?

But perhaps, Ethel, you have not got so far in your studies as to grasp a speculation like this, which is on the borderland between the physics of the body and the metaphysics of the soul.

No matter, my dear ; the bird that carols in the sky may not understand the nature of its larynx or vocal chords, but it sings all the same. And when the violin is in your hands, it is enough for you that the vague, oppressive feelings which sometimes almost stifle you seem released and soar into the summer heavens like happy birds, and that others about you thrill to your joy or your sweet imaginative pain and move about with you ' in worlds not realised.'

Now, Ethel, do not rest upon your gift. If you want to improve, and you have the artist's soul, there are but two ways. The first is real hard, even painful work. You must always begin when you take out your violin by playing some simple exercise or scale (*in tune*) until your hand aches ; then rest it, and get some one to rub it if you can, or rub it yourself, and then get it to ache again. You will thus make *giant strides* in execution, and win a facility which will surprise you in a very short time. Some people think many hours a day are wanted ; no, not many, but thorough practice—not how *long* but how *well* do you practise—attention, vigour, a certain *acharnement* as the French say, and conscientious accuracy. Accuracy before all, carefully true intonation ; so play your scales every note in exact tune, and play no faster than you can play in tune. Remember, on the piano your notes are made for you ; on the violin you have to make your own notes.

The only other counsel of perfection I will give you, as I am not here writing a manual of violin instruction, is, the best lesson you can have is to hear the great players, and catch their method of inspiration. There is no instruction like this. Wieniawski, Ernst Joachim, Sarasate, Ysaye, once heard are never forgotten, and each will leave the impress of a master's spirit upon you. Don't have a violin teacher who can't play and play well himself. Singing can be taught by people who can no longer sing—violin-playing cannot be taught except by those who can play. If your master is worth anything he will play a good deal to you—this takes time. Violin lessons ought to be much longer than piano or singing lessons, and every violin teacher worthy of the name will not count his minutes.

I am writing this paper chiefly for you, Ethel. I know Emily, your friend, is a fine pianiste

though a little too mechanical ; and Sophie has
a lovely voice, though she is a little slovenly and
slap dash.　I intend to write my next paper for
them, but I dwell on the violin first, because
girls have gone crazy about it, and I would fain
check the presumptuous ones, and encourage to
the utmost those who like you have the power
and the will to excel.

Now, a word about your instrument.　Choose
it under competent advice, of course, but choose
as you would choose a husband for yourself.
There are many very good men—but not for you ;
and there are many very good fiddles—but they
may not be for *you*.　Remember you have
got to live with this fiddle, to handle it, to be
at close quarters with it, to confide to it your
moods and feelings, to converse with it freely,
even to tend it and nurse it sometimes ; for it is
very sensitive, capricious, too, wants keeping in
good order, resents neglect—is, in fact, more like
a living thing than a manufactured article.
Don't take blindly any violin your teacher wants
you to buy.　Most teachers begin first by per-
suading you that what you have got is not good,
and then that they can sell you or choose for
you something better ; on such sales they, of
course, get large commissions—cruelly large

commissions—but you do not always benefit by
the transaction. The scale of prices which may
guide you will run thus : £5, £30, £50, £100,
£300, £1500, but you need not go beyond £1000,
unless you *will* have a unique *spécialité*, either
in condition or quality, of Stradivarius or Joseph
Guarnerius. Personally I would rather have a
good new French fiddle made at Mirecourt, or
an English £10 fiddle by Hill, than a poor
Cremona for £50. But the taste for an old-
looking fiddle (which has, alas! been copiously
flattered by whole schools devoted to forgery) is
no doubt respectable. Now, mark my words,
when a fiddle is brought to you, Ethel, although
you don't know much about fiddles, *judge for
yourself* and have only what you like. You have
got to have your hand constantly round its
neck—is the neck comfortable, or is it too
thick, so that your fingers can't reach well over
the finger-board. Does the violin *fit* you? Is
it too large, or not large enough? Can you get
at its sound? Do you like its sound? Oh yes,
it sounds well enough when your master plays
it, but it requires more strength of finger and
bow than you have got. You can't do it justice,
it sounds sulky in your hands. 'Poor little
thing!' it seems to say, 'you can't tackle me ;

it would take two of such as you to get my
sound out.' But here is a smaller pattern violin,
not so powerful—an Amati. The Amati is,
after all, the ladies' violin—Nicolas Amati, of
course, if you have £100 to spare, and can
pick one up. It is so sweet, so sensitive,
whispers almost before the bow touches the
strings, seems always on the *qui vive* to be
touched! This is the fiddle for you, Ethel;
you will be able to speak through it. Then have
regard to different qualities of tone—the shrill
Stainer, the soft Amati, the loud Joseph, the
bell-like Strad, the mellow Gzancino, the powerful Duke—every girl will feel what quality attracts
her and is sympathetic to her nature, and she
alone must decide, she must choose for herself.

And now, Ethel, a last word—don't be selfish,
don't be priggish. You have this glorious gift;
you also have in the violin an immense power
of giving pleasure to others. Don't give in to the
cant of so many musicians—'I don't feel inclined
—no inspiration—can't play,'—there's something
in it, but not much. It may not be exactly
the audience you want, but if it is an audience
that wants you, why, your higher motive comes
in there, your music and your morals. Play to
the poor not what bores them, but what they

like.   Play to please others, not always yourself.
Play to the old people who don't like Wagner,
and then don't play the Prieslied—Walter's song
from the Meistersinger—find something more
like an Italian melody of the Bellini or Rossini
type, and don't despise even old-fashioned fire-
works like the Carnival or the Cuckoo solo,
which you no longer appreciate, but which gives
such keen delight to less advanced hearers.   It
is not only foolish and priggish, but it is wrong
to take a pride in withholding what would give
so much pleasure, and which you can give with
so small an effort, just because it does not tickle
your own fancy.   And play to the sick and the
sad, and to those whose lives have little emotion
and little pleasure in them.   But I shall return
to this suggestive side of my subject, the ministry
of music to the suffering.

Enough for the present, my dear Ethel.   Remember that above the artist is the woman, and
beyond gifts are graces, and more than talent is
goodness, so that it may be written of you,
' When the eye saw me it gave witness to me ;
when the ear heard me, then it blessed me '
(Job xxix, 11).

More
Musical
Girls

MORE
MUSICAL
GIRLS

THE piano! What mixed feelings does that
word evoke! Tears at school, when the little
brain has grown weary, and there seems to the
heavy eyes no conceivable relation between the
cruel black notes on their monotonous five lines
and the white and black keys that should re-
spond to them!

The piano! A thin partition wall in a jerry-
built house, four girls on the other side, all of
whom have 'to practise.' Sometimes Herz,
sometimes Czerny, sometimes Cramer, or the
Moonlight Sonata—it matters little what, for
'tis always, 'Try again,' 'Wrong!' and *da capo*.

'But I've got to play the piano,' you say.
Very well, my dear, that is all right; some one
must suffer besides yourself, though that may
be small comfort to you; 'and since we must
all of us play' ('die,' I believe, is in the original
distich), 'let us all be unhappy together.'

But Ellen says, 'I'm serious, I'm not joking; I want advice:' and perhaps so says mamma too.

Well, then, as I observed in my first paper, it is well that all girls should play to a certain extent; and if they are not really musical, this will no doubt involve some inconvenience and unpleasantness to themselves and others. But since the benefits of being able to play even a little are substantial, and may add to a girl's usefulness in the parish, the schoolroom, and the drawing-room as life goes on, we must not hastily taboo the piano, which may prove an honest enough beast of burden, though it fall short of a racer. My excellent Polly, never mind if you can't play like Emily; every one can't have the same gifts. But do you remember the other day, when there was that party of children, and the conjurer did not turn up, and Mrs Spillikins was at her wits' end to know what to do with them? Emily was there—oh yes! But no one dared ask the solo pianist of the local Philharmonic Society to play quadrilles and polkas. The solo pianist did not offer; but, Polly, *you* did, and you soon set them all dancing, and made thirty little people happy for an hour and a half, and earned the eternal gratitude of good Mrs Spillikins.

As for Emily, she retired to talk Wagner and Bayreuth with Herr Grindlewald, and they were found in the summer-house about five o'clock, having been of no use to any one but each other —and perhaps to each other of doubtful use. Grindlewald, though a genius, was, as we all know, impecunious, and always smelling of tobacco. But there, we have no right to pry into other people's affairs—in or out of summer-houses. Still, we must own, Polly, you did score that afternoon, though you played most vilely. You felt very happy, all the same, and made a good many more happy too.

Still, Emily, it is girls like you I want to have a chat with just now. You have a fine musical organisation. Your mother wanted you to play the harp—it was fashionable in her youth, and if a girl had a willowy sort of back it was supposed to show off her arms. But you resisted this, along with the guitar, mandoline, zither, banjo, and all such spasmodic eccentricities of fashion. The cool white keys of a grand pianoforte smiled to you from early childhood; you surprised your teachers by the ease with which you surmounted the difficulties and drudgeries of the early stages. When you were only eight, the organist called and played

some songs without words, and your great
wondering eyes devoured him, whilst your
little ears got deliciously, bewilderingly thrilled
with the magic music, and when he had gone,
'I want to play like that man,' you said it to your
mother, and the next day you said again, and
nothing would do but '*that man*' had to be sent
for. Ah, little eight-year-old! he was your first
love, though you never knew it. Poor Mr
Satterlee! he was very, very kind to you, he
taught you on and off for three years. You
made wonderful progress—you were a prodigy,
Emily. He even taught you to play some of
the easier Chopin's. At last he couldn't teach
you any more,—he was dying of consumption,—
but loved to have you go round to him; and as
he lay on his sofa, looking so pale and worn,
with those wonderful bright eyes, and that
irresistible but rather sad smile, he would hear
you play, and give you what hints he could,
moving his thin, delicate hand to beat time.
He called you his sunshine, and you illumined
him out of the world. No sweeter, purer spirit
than gentle Mr Satterlee's ever cherished ideal
aspirations whilst on earth, and when his eager
soul took flight it was like a sigh of music

escaping to rejoin the celestial harmonies from whence it came.

Happy the girl who has had such a master, and caught from such a gifted and pure genius her earliest musical aspirations. You are nineteen now, Emily; you can pronounce slap-dash judgments on the new singers, and use all the Bayreuth slang, and turn up your nose at everyone who does not belong to your special musical '*ism*,' and all that ; but there is one spot in your country churchyard at home where every spring the violets are fresh, and on one day in the year you never forget to hang your wreath of fresh flowers upon a certain marble cross. You are quite right, my dear, I honour you for it ; for you owe to him who lies beneath the deepest art impulses of your life.

No doubt, Emily, you have attained a degree of excellence which is seldom found in this country. Your snare is the 'Sturm und Drung' school. Don't be the slave of technique—it is ruining music. It is easier to be a fast than a feeling player. The great masters, like Liszt, Thalberg, Rubinstein, excelled in expression as well as in pace, but their followers imitate too frequently what, in fact, they are alone capable of copying—the *technique*—forgetting that technique is nothing but a means to an end.

Rubinstein's later pianoforte compositions are little else but bravura exercises, so hard and heartless, and so difficult, we almost wish they were impossible. Chopin and Schumann were great writers of bravura passages—so was Mendelssohn when he chose—but in their music sentiment is never sacrificed to execution, beauty and passion to noise and astonishment.

Study the 'Songs without Words' and the Mendelssohn Concertos, now too seldom heard ; but above all, seek to play in concerted music, string, quintet, and quartet, and with the orchestra whenever you can. Of course, Emily, your music is so exceptional that it amounts to a vocation ; and you are right, like any highly gifted artistic person, to spend a good deal of time and attention upon it. It is your special gift to the society in the midst of which you move, but it need not make you selfish ; you need not be ashamed of stooping to conquer. I remember Liszt once at Edinburgh was forbidden by his contract to play out of the concert room, and visiting a quiet family, who were eagerly bent upon hearing him, at last sat down to the piano, and said, 'Now, young ladies, I must not play to be *heard*, as at a concert, but I am not forbidden to play for those who want to dance. So, if you will dance, I will play as long as ever you dance.' And for an hour or more the young people danced, whilst the great master improvised such quadrilles and waltzes as had never probably been heard before or since.

No virtuosity, my dear Emily, should make you too grand to be kind and good-natured.

There are pianoforte-playing girls of all degrees, and I must dismiss them with a few general hints.

If you are real music lovers you will gain an immense deal of pleasure from learning to read music fluently and *à quatres mains*. Almost every composition, orchestral or choral, of any note, has been set for four hands. And this form not only familiarises you with a vast range of music, but the association with another all the while is delightful—providing the other happens to be delightful.

Rise early, and play your scales before breakfast, major and minor. I know it is an old fashion, and many devices have been invented to supersede it ; but sometimes, as the poet has sung, 'old ways are best.'

Then you should give your freshest, not your

jaded energies to the piano; and you are, or ought to be, freshest in the morning,—the morning for preparation, the night for results. The morning is for method and judgment; the night for the senses, the emotions, and the imagination.

Be not a sloven in your practising any more than in your dressing; don't tolerate false notes and leave others to fall foul of them.

Of course you cannot play your best when people are talking, but you cannot always refuse to play because people are rude or insensible to your merits. Keep a stock of short pieces; a little will satisfy those who don't want anything, and you will avoid being disobedient or disobliging.

One thing I should like to say to most girls who play *and sing*. When you have discovered your voice, don't be in such a desperate hurry to cleave to an accomplishment which you justly hold will bring you more fame and attention as to abandon your piano practice. If you do what most girls do, neglect their piano when they begin to sing, you will cease to play your own accompaniments accurately.

Sophie has a pretty soprano, but having more ear for melody than harmony—the way with all half-taught musicians—she thinks any chords

near the mark will do ; nor does a false chord or
note in the bass distress her, and sooner than
get it right she will leave it out altogether.

I wish I could make Sophie feel that although
I quite appreciate her vocal facility, her song
with the 'smudged' accompaniment gives me no
pleasure whatever ; it makes me angry. She not
only insults her composer, but puts an affront
upon her audience, whilst cheapening herself.
This peculiar defect, so common and so often
unrebuked, is the hardest to get a girl to notice
or to remedy. Sophie is really incorrigible ; I
have left off asking her to sing.

Queenie, you are better. I like your singing
very much. Your voice is rich, and you have
'tears in your throat,' as Mario used to say ;
but although you seldom play false notes, you
don't master your accompaniments so completely
as not to be obliged to think about your notes.
This constantly checks your emotion, for if you
are thinking about the next bar of accompaniment, it is so much off the spontaneous feeling
you have to spare for the melody you are singing.
You should be able to play your accompaniment
almost with your eyes shut (as I have heard
Rubenstein play divinely in the dark) before
ever you attempt to sing to it. Of course, if

you can get some one to play for you, well and
good, for you will usually sing better standing
up.

Now about the training of your voice. If
you have real musical sensibility and an unmanageable organ, it may be worth cultivating ; but
if you have a defective ear and even a good
voice with some sensibility, I would not advise
you to attempt singing at all. It is wonderful
how much can be done in disciplining a voice,
but not if you had a bad ear. Trebelli's voice
was most unmanageable, but she had a rare
dramatic and musical gift and an exquisite ear,
and she worked her voice at last into wonderful
evenness and flexibility.

Some sing very sweetly in their own way,
and seem spoiled by a little training. There is
sometimes a danger of losing the *spécialité*
which pleases without winning the excellence
which excites admiration. Great care should
be taken in selecting your teacher ; but if you
are really musical, one or two lessons will suffice
to show you whether you have found the right
professor. It does not follow that the teacher
that did wonders for Alice is equally good for
Queenie. Queenie doesn't like him, or she can
never fix her attention upon what he says, or

she is thinking all the time of *him* and not of his *instruction*, or she is wool-gathering.

Sometimes an unpretending teacher, who wins and understands her, and can make her attend and understand, and above all, inspires her to work, is far more efficacious than another with a great name at a guinea for half-an-hour.

Aurelia, my dear, you are a born queen of song; still you would not do on the stage, and you are not heavy enough for oratorio, but for the sympathetic ballad of the Chaminade school, for the German *lied*, the French *chanson* (words by De Musset), the music of Gounod or Bizet, the English romance of Arthur Sullivan, the sentimental fancy of Tosti, you are incomparable; in fact, you 'charm.' What voices, abilities, achievements in vocal music do we constantly meet with, but 'without charm!' You have that incommunicable thing, the *émotion voilée, une voix sympathique*, and just the magnetism which comes from the heart and goes to the heart.

Aurelia, your gift is great, so is your responsibility. You will thrill refined audiences; don't despise touching homely hearts too. Think of the pleasure and peace you ;can bring to the careworn and the suffering, of the joy and ex-

D

hilaration you can shed amongst the poor, in the workhouse, the hospital, the village school-room; consider the gracious ministry which your music may bring to bedridden sufferers cut off from the external world and all opportunities of social enjoyment.

'But,' you say, 'I don't find these people or come upon these opportunities.'

Of course you don't, for you never seek them, nor are you in the way when wanted; nor ready — 'the readiness is all,' as Hamlet remarks. Most of the things left undone for which we ask forgiveness in church are so from sheer thoughtlessness. It is wonderful how many kindnesses a feeling heart finds to do, how many needs a willing hand knows how to supply.

And lastly, my dear Aurelia, you who are made much of, and are in request, remember that brilliant gifts need not make you neglect wholesome duties. Your mother wants you, so do your brother, your sisters, and others who may be less fortunate and less happy than you are. The service you owe them may be even good for yourself; it may counteract any temptation to morbid tendencies and to that ennui which the routine of success seldom fails to bring. The expansion of your moral and affectionate nature through daily but loving sacrifice may actually purify your artistic nature, and prevent you becoming *selfish*, not to say perilously *sensuous*. Remember that we are placed here, none of us 'to live unto ourselves, or to die unto ourselves, and that although it may be right and fit to devote yourself ardently to the cultivation of your own special gifts and to rejoice in the exercise of them, concerning all such is written, 'These ought ye to have done ;' but in view of those many duties which belong to you as a girl in her home, surrounded by a girl's common duties and responsibilities, please do not forget the end of Christ's admonition, 'not to leave the other undone.'

Parochial
Girls

PAROCHIAL
GIRLS

SOME girls seem born to bend circumstances to their will, others have to adapt themselves to circumstances ; we all have to do the latter more or less—generally more. But, happily, we are like indiarubber, we can be stretched and twisted ; like indiarubber, too, we have a tendency to return to our original shape.

The happiness of life, my dear restless, dreamy Eleanor,—so fond of change, with little fixity of purpose, but with such a kind heart at the bottom, and so much capacity were it only directed and enthused,—the happiness of life is not always to have your own way, or to gratify the passing whim, but to find out what you were sent into this world to do, and wherever you are to do as much of it as you can ; and if you can't do what you like, you must try and like what you have got to do. There is no lot in life in which some, perhaps most, of our best faculties cannot be drawn out and made to tell, if only we are sufficiently unselfish, sufficiently observant, and sufficiently willing to work.

The real hindrance to your happiness, if you only knew it, is a craving for something different from what you have, instead of making the most of what you have got. Remember, 'unto him that hath shall be given.' To use to the utmost your present opportunities is the only sure stepping-stone to something better.

I once knew two boys engaged in sweeping out the same warehouse, but one thought the job a little beneath him, and whilst dreaming of a more dignified position higher up in the establishment, for which he thought his birth and talents qualified him, scamped his work, and always seemed to do what he did grudgingly—'*Gentleman Jones*,' he was nicknamed. The other, always cheery and bright, worked away with a will, as if to get the place clean and tidy were the only thing in life worth doing. Now, although his father had never been a nobleman's butler or received a fiver from the Prince of Wales, and honest Brown was only a labourer's son educated at a Board school, still when the

time came, the head clerk looked at the two
boys, and slipped Brown, not 'Gentleman Jones,'
into the ticket-desk ; whereupon Jones resigned
in disgust, and has not got another place yet !

Now, Eleanor, there are three of you girls.
Your father has a large suburban parish, your
mother is rather an invalid. Susan, the elder
girl, is twenty-four ; she manages the house-
keeping, the penny bank, the clothing club,
being quick at figures, and with quite a gift
for order and organisation,—you have very little
gift for either. Susan also teaches in the
Sunday school, but not very well, her mind
being so much more practical than thoughtful
or reflective. You are somewhat better fitted
for that, but you won't focus your mind, and
don't like working under direction. You are
just nineteen. You will never have Rachel's
gifts ; she is dramatic and musical, hates figures,
and doesn't take very kindly to Sunday school;
but she is splendid with the boys, and invaluable
at choir practices or school feasts. She is the
popular one, no doubt ; but because you cannot
be Rachel, don't sit down with your hands before
you, Eleanor. You can be something which
neither Rachel nor Susan are born to be. Come
out of your trance, dreamy Eleanor. The world

is not a hollow show or an empty vision, but a great business mart—a place of endless gains and losses—in which every one has a stall to keep or a stake to win, and a niche to fill. Find your niche! It is partly marked out for you by your character, partly by your environment.

And here I come to the point—*your* point. That vague dreaminess, that ardent imagination, that warm but shyly affectionate temperament which gives you away when you least know it, and reveals secrets which you would most wish to keep, that tell-tale colour that comes and goes beyond your control, the quick scorn or melting tenderness, the little broken sentence that slips out and half reveals and half conceals your meaning, and the sensitive expressions which flit across your face like the shine and shadow upon upland hills, and make it a very tell-tale dial of the soul that leaps and flutters beneath—this, and a great deal more, Eleanor, bears witness to character gifts and psychological peculiarities which are the sources of your *power*, but which are now like diffused steam—wasted in mere vapour.

You want your emotions concentrated; you want your energies focused and directed. That is what your environment can do for you, if you

will be wise, and try to think a little more of
others and less about yourself.

You are getting morbidly self-conscious,
Eleanor — fastidious, discontented. But the
world was not made only for you ; it is a mixed
world, a suffering world, a sinful world, and
you are there to make it less sorrowful, less
confused, better. But you can only do this by
making *yourself* better, and you can only become
better by doing what you are fitted to do—
using your Talent. The Master has not said,
'dream,' 'speculate,' 'grumble,' 'idle,'—but
'*occupy* till I come.'

So then, Eleanor, you are at present thought
to be the least useful of the girls, and are
admired and made much more of away from
home than in your own parish. Now, my dear,
you have got to concentrate and discover your
vocation just *where you are*. You will not have
far to seek. That young housemaid who has
come from a distance is homesick. This is her
first place ; the cook is a little hard on her,
your mother expects everything done as usual,
and the girl gets taken up short and scolded
for not doing as a matter of course, what she
did not understand she was to do. Practical
Susan thinks she had better go—inexperienced

young things are such a bother. Brilliant
Rachel thinks it quite simple—if one servant
does not suit, try another. You find the child—
for she is little more—in tears. At a flash your
intuitive, imaginative nature seizes the situation,
and your kind heart does the rest. You think
of how she is alone in the world for the first
time—no mother or teacher to go to for a word
of advice or encouragement—of the disappointment, perhaps injury to her, of a hasty dismissal
—of the scolding at home—of her ignorance of
what to do—of her pitiful sense of injustice at
being chided for not doing what she had not
been told to do, and sent off without a fair trial
—of her discouragement, and sense of failure,
and feeling of stupidity (she is rather a bright
girl) at being *thought* stupid—for people are apt
to become what we think them.

You don't go through this analysis deliberately.
The instant you find the child crying to herself
as she is hanging out the clothes to dry in the
kitchen garden, and hear the cook's harsh voice,
'Where have you got to now?—didn't I tell
you?' etc. etc.,—you feel it all in a flash, and
presently you go to the girl, and, patting her on
the shoulder, you say, 'Cheer up, Annie; it
will be all right by and by. And if you want

to know anything, just come to me and I will
tell you. I am sure you will get on very nicely
when you understand our ways ; it will take a
day or two, you know, and I will speak to
mother for you. Have you heard from your
own mother ? I suppose you can write—or shall
I write for you, and tell her that I think you
will do very well, and that you like your place ? '
' Oh, please, miss,' says poor Cinderalla, ' I am
sure you're very kind, miss ; and if I only knew
what to do, I am sure I would try '—and a little
sob chokes Cinderella as she hides herself behind
a piece of underlinen which she stands on tiptoe
to hang on the clothes-line. And this little act
of thoughtful kindness which you were fitted to
do, and do so gracefully, brings its reward. From
that moment Cinderella becomes your abject
slave. Cinderella keeps her place ; and by and
by, when you marry the squire's son, and a
smart, pretty maid, with a little heart beating
perhaps faster than yours, follows your bridal
carriage to the station in charge of your personal
luggage, why, who is it but Cinderella, who is
to be your faithful lady's-maid, and who, all
for love of you, will not listen to M. Jules, the
fascinating head waiter at the *Hotel des Fiancées*

'on the Continong,' and whose father has vine-
yards in the South—'Sapristi!'

Ah, Eleanor, if you only knew it, what lovely
conquests,—what happy, ay, blessed conquests,
—you could go through the world making, by
placing that rare, sensitive, intuitive nature of
yours at the disposal of others, instead of allowing it to dissipate in vague and perhaps not very
wholesome daydreams.

Yours, too, is a presence whom the sick would
learn to bless.   You have perhaps never discovered what Guinevere found out so late—too
late in her wild and tragic life—'the gentle
power of ministration' in you.   You are not
partial to sickrooms or to suffering—probably
not.   Well, you will get to love them, when you
feel by the smile on the pale face as you enter,
the grateful tear when you depart, that the
sound of your feet is as the soft tread of an
angel on the threshold of the afflicted, and the
touch of your cool, magnetic hand like the
balsam of God upon the fevered brow.   You
need not talk religion, but your sweet 'May I
come in?' and the eager reply, 'Ay, missy, you
be always welcome ; and thankee for the flowers,
and for the syrup, it were a lovely drink. And sit
ve doon and talk. And how be your lady mither?

and we's no' heard or seen her of late. Now, Betsy, take the young lady's parasol, and run into the garden and pick yon big strawberries, they be just ripe. Maybe, miss, ye ha' mair and better; but these be ourn, and we wad love ye to tak' some, and I might mak' sae bold.'

And that poor boy, Eleanor, who will never rise again, and whose one hour in life that is full of heaven is just when you come and read him those tales of travel, and tell him about the village sports he will never join in any more. You have positively developed and refined and poetised his soul, you have advanced him in moral and mental progress, so that when he starts again on the other side of what we call death, he will start from a higher platform, and move in more celestial air.

And at times you seem curiously magnetic. People say you cure them. Yours is a sort of reviving, healing presence. You have only to sit at their bedsides and they feel better; you hold their hands, and make them strong. The touch of your light, taper fingers in their hair, your hand upon their brow, eases pain and diffuses comfort. You can put the sufferer to sleep, and he or she will wake strangely re-freshed. This is your gift, and it carries your

love with it—the love of the human in all—the
pity of Christ. You may not feel bound to talk
religion to them; the Rev. Thomas Gabriel no
doubt has a gift that way, and the people do not
resent his spiritual attentions because of the
kindly earnestness of his manner. But your
sphere is somewhat different. You are weighted
with no professional responsibilities ; with you it
is the ' one touch of nature makes the whole
world kin.' So, Eleanor, you see now what I
mean by getting yourself focused. Some natures
grow like careless garden weeds, and run to seed.
You are a great deal too good for that. And
let me tell you that vague, dreamy, imaginative,
and poetically unpractical as you seem to be,
you will never be happy until you are thoroughly
useful ; nor will you be able to make a man
happy, or be fit to have a family of your own,
unless as an unmarried girl you learn to forget
yourself, and give yourself to others.

Although, like most girls of your peculiar
temperament, you are not so interesting to your
family as you are to outsiders, you are far more
subtle and complex than either Rachel, your
artistic sister, or Susan, who is the practical
Martha of the family.

People find it more difficult to manage you,

and you find it difficult to manage yourself; though whenever you apply yourself to the task, you do not find it difficult to manage other people. They have a feeling that you are on a distinctly different plane, and in some sense a higher plane, and you influence them in spite of themselves to do your bidding, and condone your idiosyncrasies, which they are apt to call faults, or at least *peculiarities*.

For all these reasons I have given you more consideration than I need bestow on Rachel or Susan.

Now, Rachel, you are in danger of being spoilt. You go up and stay with friends in London. Those little bright songs you sing make you a favourite at bazaars and fancy fairs, and in polite drawing-rooms, too, when people are worn-out with Tosti and De Lara sentiment. Oh, you can do that too. You are a born artiste, and there is nothing you would like better than going on the stage; but your father, who is a rural dean, objects.

When you come back you look languidly upon those triumphs at the penny readings, when your recitation and song episode used to be considered worth all the money, and you were intoxicated with thunders of applause, not un-

E

mixed with stampings, whistlings and shoutings, which now (must I own it?) you a little despise. Self again, my dear Rachel. What you have loved and lived for all along hitherto is yourself, and this new apathy convicts you.

Now, my dear Rachel, that way lies such a fatal disenchantment with life as seeks ever stronger and stronger stimulants, until the whole head is sick and the whole heart is faint. You too have to learn that to live for others is the only way to keep the heart fresh and the sensibilities keen. You have got to unfold yourself and fill out the sphere of your daily life to the utmost. You had quite a gift for boys, just as Susan has for girls. Your boys' class in the Sunday school was always full, and you ruled them easily, not because you had any very strong grip of the religious doctrine you had to inculcate, but because the nucleus of your class consisted of the choir boys. You had a rare gift of teaching music, and then they delighted in the entertainments you organised for them, and so it happened that wherever you went, and whatever you did or said or taught, seemed wonderful in their eyes. The little fellows raved about you, and brought you ripe plums; and the big ones presented you with an illumi-

nated round robin of thanks, accompanied by
a remarkable letter, in which respect and
emotion wrestled not always successfully with
grammar and orthography, but which you had
framed and hung up in your bedroom.

It is not a good sign in you, Rachel, to feel a
little ashamed of that gorgeous illumination now.
The days of your childish glee in your early
triumphs may have gone by. You are twenty,
at the summit of your girlhood's freshness and
beauty. You can do what you like with those
young fellows. Will you throw such an opportunity away? Won't you make a stand for
Temperance? Won't you help them to organise
recreations for themselves which will counteract
vicious excitements? Won't you make your
much-prized favour the reward of the honest,
the industrious, the steady? What an influence
you are when you pass down the High Street!
From your smile or coldness not one of those
hobbledehoys but what knows your mind
towards him, and carries home the perfume of
your goodwill or the rankling sting of your
displeasure.

So, Rachel, you become a power in your
suburban parish for good, and is not this an
ambition worthy of you? Don't be cheated

out of it by the glamour of scented drawing-
rooms and the smiles and sophistries of polite
gallants.

And now, dear Susan, you think I am leaving
you out in the cold. But no. You can do what
neither Rachel or Eleanor are in the least fit to
excel in. Without the machinery you supply,
the order, regularity, organising power, quick-
ness of practical insight and fertile resource
which belong to you and to no one else in the
parish to anything like the same extent, how
restricted would the spheres of your two sisters
be, how futile much of your father's labour, how
terrible your mother's anxieties ! To know that
the penny bank is right because you are there,
that the tradesmen's bills are receipted because you
had the money, that father will miss no engagement because you keep his diary, that the best
school prizes will be bought for the least money,
that the supply of milk at the school feast will
not run short, and that there will be no confusion in the entertainments, and no dissatisfac-
tion at the awards, because you with your staff of
lieutenants—the young ladies of the congrega-
tion who move unquestioningly at your bidding,
the young gentlemen who rush at a look or a
word of command with perfect confidence in,

and no small admiration for, your brain, firmness, and absolute command of the situation—is this not a noble sphere, until something wider still opens for you ?

Susan, you are born to be a statesman's wife, nor will it be difficult for you to transfer that tact, good-humour, firmness, and inexhaustible resource to any station of life to which it may please God to call you.

So, my dear girls, the parish is a kingdom, and you are the governors. Why should you not all combine to make it 'the kingdom of Christ'?

Learned
Girls

LEARNED
GIRLS

'JACK says he does not think women ought to be educated too much, what's the good of it to them?'

'Nonsense!' says mamma, who has lately gone in for the higher education of women, University Extension lectures and the Franchise. 'All boys talk this kind of stuff about girls. Pray how old is Cousin Jack?'

'Oh, he's of age, you know—twenty-one last May.'

'Quite old enough to know better.'

'Well, mamma,' says Juliet, who's got a great opinion of Jack, 'I don't think I like being highly educated myself.'

'You're not, my dear,' says mamma rather tartly; 'hitherto all attempts to develop your mind have conspicuously failed.'

'Perhaps I have not got a mind, mamma. But I get along just as well as most girls. I danced every dance the other night at Lady Fitzmagigs, and Jack said I was what he called a 'whale on ices,' and I made him furiously jealous of Captain Popinjay before the end of the evening.'

'And that's what you call "getting along"! Juliet, you're hopeless! And just as I've paid for a new course of Professor Blinkum's University Extensions on the Scandinavian coleoptera!'

Juliet, who is a merry black-eyed little brunette, just turned seventeen, looks penitent, but not convinced; she feels she has said something dreadful, but she does not know what, so she comes up to her mother and puts her arms round her neck, and lays her fresh blooming cheek sideways on her mother's.

'Look here, you dear darling mumsey wumsey, it's no use pretending I care about the Scandinavian coleoptera—send Norah instead—and get me a bike, that's a dear precious spoilt cross mamma, and I'll be so good, and weed all day in the garden, which I don't mind, and sweep out the tool house, which I hate doing.'

Somehow Juliet always melted her rather strenuous and zealous educational mother, who had lately visited Girton, and had adopted theories about higher education (her own had been somewhat neglected) ; but mamma's rather sudden zeal for learning had not dried up a fund of warm-heartedness and good-nature, which Juliet seemed always to know how to get at, with her merry ways and her transparent candour ; whilst—must it be admitted ?—the more sedate and learned Norah, aged nineteen, was not nearly so much in favour, and, I grieve to say, frequently in the sulks, though very assiduous at her lessons.

In general society Norah was rather glum—not bad-looking, but glum. She did not fall in with games, or ever clap her hands, or go into fits of merriment like Juliet, or care to amuse children, or put herself out for any one. She did not like boating—she liked long walks with some one who did not want her to talk much ; but she could always listen, only then you could not be quite sure whether she was attending to you ; her answers were usually brief and not very suggestive. Some people thought she was shy ; but Professor Blinkum said, after she had been through the course neglected by Juliet, that her Scandinavian paper was wonderful, and she must have a prodigious memory ; and yet although she stored facts and phrases—for a time, at least—she was not good at an essay, and never by any chance emitted an idea or reflection she had not heard from somebody else, or read in some book. Still, most people admitted that Norah was very learned. It was wonderful what she knew when it came to an examination on paper, but no one would have gathered this from her monosyllabic conversation, in which she never seemed to give out anything ; but then there was something so lofty and superior about her silence, and she had such an evident contempt for those who were not under 'higher education,' that people were usually impressed, and in very much the same way. They said, ' Wonderfully clever ! so learned, you know—and (but this was not always uttered) so dull ! ' And it was true ! Somehow, Norah was a mistake, with all her knowledge. Norah should have developed in a different way, and then she would have been all right, or at least more right than she was. Her mind should have been a little more let alone and her heart a little more moved, and her timid rudimentary sympathies a little more drawn forth in childhood ; but not being very attractive, she was rather mulct of the affection which she most needed.

In her early girlhood she was reserved and a little prim, although there was a dash of angular

decision about her, and it was certain she had
a will of her own ; but she was singularly
unemotional, hardly ever cried, and only laughed
under protest. She seemed afraid of spontaneity
and self-revelation of any kind, but she doubtless
had energy and purpose. She collected postage
stamps at nine with avidity, then she had a
perfect craze for picking up pins, removing
orange peel from the pavement, and collecting
windfalls in autumn—heaps of windfalls, which
the cook made into pies. She liked the garden,
and on wet days she used to read almanacs full
of dates and events, but never opened a story-
book. At school her progress in arithmetic was
wonderful, and she did her sums twice as fast
as the teacher at the blackboard, and thus
became the envy of the class and a terror to
the young mistress fresh from the training
college. She seemed to have a squirrel-like
capacity for acquiring but acquiring, quite
mechanically, and her prehensile mind would
lay hold of anything, store it, and then—do
nothing with it.

Poor Norah seemed to want friends, but she
had no power of winning them. If she had
warm sympathies, she was so shy of them that
at last they got overlaid and stifled with dates,

arithmetic, and coleoptera. As she grew older
she developed a certain intensity, and threw
herself with a sort of mental desperation upon
her class studies.   Of originality, thought, power,   .
she seemed to have none ; but she accumulated
to such an extent that she was perfectly
suffocated with facts that she could neither
arrange nor interpret, and information that she
could neither assimilate nor reproduce except
at examinations.

Norah was one of those girls who pass through
their youth with a barren reputation for ability
—no one quite knows why, or what for.   Perhaps
she was never quite happy out of the class-room ;
for there, with all the energy of her isolated and
hungry intelligence she was taking in facts,
which, when the examination came on, she
would take a singular pride in putting out
again in heaps in neat little unopened packets,
just as they had been taken in.

You feel inclined to leave off reading about
Norah, my dear.

'Poor Norah!' you say. 'I like Juliet much
better.   Your Norah bores me.' Yes, and she
bores other people, and bores herself too.   But
wait a bit. I have an object in sketching
Norah—first, because this chapter is about

learned girls ; and secondly, because all learned
girls are not like Norah. Norah is a type—
rather a sad type—of the learned girl. Would
you like to see how Norah ends ? Norah will
never marry. There was just one chance, one
man, but it never came off—it never really quite
came on—but there was for at least six months
an unusual, an alarming flutter in Norah's almost
impenetrable breast. One evening *he* left the
garden, and turned as he went down the lane.
But Norah never turned to look at him, or
wave adieu ; her features were rigid, and her
poor heart, somewhere beneath its ice-bound
covering, was almost breaking, or as near breaking as such a heart, beneath such a covering,
could be. Then *he* lighted a cigar, and muttering,
' Not a bit of use,' gulped down something like
a sob, and the next day he left for Egypt, and
he never saw her again.

Every girl has her serious romance, and that
was yours, Norah, and you never had another.

You were a difficult girl for a romance. Your
pent-up nature will lavish itself henceforth upon
neither men, women, nor children. You would
prove an admirable secretary to some Herbert
Spencer, Darwin, or an assistant-librarian—anything connected with the accumulation and

tabulation of detail—but you will always want direction, some one to do the thinking for you, and then you will slave like a cart horse. Your education has never taught you to think. Shall I indulge in speculation and look for a moment with a prophetic eye into the future? Your emotional nature, developing capriciously and too late, will lavish itself wildly on pet dogs or cats, and you will keep birds and pigeons, and your garden in the country will be neatly edged with innumerable cockle shells, and you will know the Latin name for every flower in the garden, but few will know that you know. You will be good to the poor out of a sense of duty, but they won't care much about you, and the village children will bob curtseys to you out of sheer terror, and you will be known as 'old Miss Norah,' and always wear black silk, summer and winter, and go to church regularly, and leave your money to a hospital.

· · · · · ·

There was no one like Irene at lawn tennis. The breeze, as she ran or rather floated about the smooth lawn, toyed with her bright hair that made a sort of floss silk nimbus about her pure forehead, her quick blue eyes flashed with merriment : but she played the game with rapt

attention, and that spontaneous correlation of
mind and body which in such exercises means
perfect grace. Yet there was nothing *farouche*
or sternly preoccupied about her playing such
as you may observe in people who lose their
tempers over a stroke at croquet or billiards or a
move at chess, or those others who impute every
disaster that happens to them at whist to their
partners in the game ; and Irene could toss back
a quick repartee over the net as well as a ball.
She seemed to get equal enjoyment out of it
whether she lost or won ; and she generally
won ; but to her it never became a solemn business—it never ceased to be a game.

When she was on the ground, no one seemed
able to take their eyes off Irene. Her supple
motions, her lithe but well developed figure, the
living expectancy of her attitude, the rapidity
and decision of her stroke, her pretty way of
running backward, and her little spring off the
ground to catch the ball, her willowy stoop and
graceful sweep, it was an education in athletics
to watch her. The women admired Irene just
as much as the men.

There is no greater aspersion on the sex than
to say that girls are always jealous, and never
admire each other's beauty. There is quite as

F

much genuine admiration between girls as there
is hero worship amongst men.

When the game was over, I saw Irene's par-
ticular girl friend, who had been making tea on
the terrace, go to meet her as she came off the
ground, a little out of breath from the last
severe tussle with Bob Clifford, the champion of
the Zebra Club. The Gloire de Dijon rose had
fallen from her bosom, only the stalk and green
leaves remained; she was still flushed with
excitement, and smiling. 'Well, I declare I
never saw anything much more "fetching," the
more so as she seemed so completely unconscious
of her own charms,' I heard Celia say, as she
twined her arm in Irene's, and the two ap-
proached the tea-table, where little groups were
assembled.

'Look here, dear, poor mother is in such a
fix. There's Monsieur le Comte de Chauvesouris
just come, and no one likes to speak French to
him, and he doesn't know a word of English. I
heard mother say to him, " Prenez-voutez ? "
" Comment, madame ? " said he. " No, not come
on ! " said mother—I don't think she knew what
she was saying, and the Count looked rather
embarrassed.' (Irene went into fits.) 'Do for
goodness' sake come on and talk French to him,

you talk it so well.' So Irene was led straight up to Monsieur le Comte and introduced. As luck or ill-luck would have it, a gilded hairpin dropped out, and a stray tress fell like a coil of golden silk across her face. She had just plucked the roseless stalk and leaves from her dress and thrown them down, and now she tried to tuck the rebellious curl back under her hat.

'Vous voyez, Monsieur le Comte,' she said, with perfect self-possession, 'je viens de jouer, et je suis tellement en désordre!'

'Mais, mademoiselle,' exclaimed the polite Comte, placing his hand on his breast with a low bow, 'vous êtes un reve!'

Presently Irene and the Count seemed quite at their ease. Irene talked French fluently. They were both great admirers of Sarah Bernhardt, and then she had been at school in Paris, and knew several of the studios. She was just eighteen, and had not long been presented at Court.

Now, Irene is a learned girl—she was always fond of books. Unlike the girls of the period, who get in all the new risky books, and read them first to see whether they are fit for the perusal of their parents, Irene actually read Walter Scott's novels for her pleasure; and her

In Memoriam was profusely marked before she was sixteen. She was also a student of George Eliot; she did not care for Dickens, but she had a great admiration for, without much sympathy with Thackeray. She loved Charlotte Brontë, brooded over Emerson, and you would often find a volume of Oliver Wendell Holmes open on her bedroom table. She was also one of the few learned girls who took Longfellow to her heart of hearts. Now, Irene had been through courses, and attended University Extension lectures. Her memory was not always as extensive as Norah's, nor had she anything like the same power of accumulating facts and registering dates; nor was arithmetic her strong point. She did not read so much, but she read to more purpose; she read, as Emerson would say, 'creatively.' She assimilated her books. She did not wear her knowledge like a charade costume which seemed not to belong to her, and to which she did not belong; but her information became part of herself, and she owned it, and knew how to use it and handle it in manifold relations. She could not quote Ruskin, but after reading the *Seven Lamps* she could stand at Amiens or Chatre and take infinite delight in traceries, statues, and points of construction, and explain why they interested her. She read *Modern Painters*, and saw the relation at once between Claude and Turner ; the contrast between both and Canaletto interested her when she went to Venice. The very old masters excited her immensely, and she could tell you clearly why they fascinated her more than some later men who drew the human form correctly and understood perspective. She had a perfect craze for Giotto, which people who did not understand her thought mere affectation ; but his eye for significant detail enthused her, and his dramatic perception of interesting moments and subtle situations, which lifts him as a spontaneous genius so far above the conventional level of his age, spoke to her imagination and touched her heart.

'Here is another by my dear Giotto,' she exclaimed, stopping before a dingy wood-panel in one of the Italian galleries, past which her friends were hurrying. 'Look, Cerise. I think it was Schlegel on Art first taught me to watch for Giotto, and he was quite right. What could be more tender and pathetic, here in this panel ? See, it is written in Latin, but the Catalogue translates it, " Jesus sayeth farewell to His friends." The executioners wait with the hammer and nails, the cross lies on the ground ready, they are just going to nail the Saviour down, but they pause, touched apparently themselves with a moment of compunction. His friends cluster round Him ; He is shaking hands with them for the last time.'

'You are right, Irene,' says Cerise, quite interested ; 'but I should have passed the dingy old panel.'

'Look at the next,' continues Irene. 'It is almost more pathetic. The Saviour is lifted now high on the cross, His mother and the beloved disciple are looking up at His bleeding feet, their faces are full of anguish ; He inclines His head towards them. The moment is chosen when He addresses St John and commits the Virgin Mary to his care—"Behold thy mother ! Behold thy son ! " and underneath is written so quaintly but tenderly, " Jesus maketh His will " ! '

Oh yes, Irene has read her art books to some purpose. She may not know so many dates, nor might she score such high marks as Norah, but she could write such an essay on Art as Norah would never understand or be able to pen a line of. And, indeed, she did so once, when she was studying at Berlin ; and the melancholy thing about it was that Professor Von Stipple, the examiner who read it merely remarked, 'Dis lady has vera mouch vat you call fancy, but she no read my book on ze technique of ze old meisters!' Now Norah would have read the book and scored many more marks.

You see, my dear young lady reader, it is possible to study too many books on 'ze technique' and other things. As a rule, I think studious people read too much and think too little. I seldom take up a book wherein the writer tells me what *he* has thought out, or what *he* really loves or has seen for himself. Everything is mincemeat nowadays. It has done duty elsewhere, in books, magazine articles, and what not. New books are mostly hashes up of old books, picture recollections of other pictures, and every one seems waiting to know what somebody else is going to say before they give an opinion about the Academy, the Salon, the last new book, the last speech in Parliament or Congress, the last play. I say, if you really mean culture, and not cram, read less and think more, copy less and design more, think your own thoughts. What, child! Has Nature nothing to say to you? are there no whispers for your ears alone? must you always be so public and common? That is not true culture, that is not education.

Culture means making something grow on your own seed-plot, not transplanting flowers in full bloom—cut flowers, too, mostly, without any roots. Education does not mean stuffing with facts under high pressure as they stuff Strasburg geese, and often with similar results, a diseased liver. Education means drawing out and not ramming in. To draw out your faculties, your sympathies, to develop your tastes, perceptions, to balance your judgment, to give you the power not only of acquiring but of using what you acquire, to enable you to see the relative importance of things, and never to mistake the means for the ends (as Christ said, What shall it profit if a man gain the whole world and lose his own soul?), that is culture.

You will see by this time that Irene, the learned girl's mind, was very active. Once she tried science, and was much interested in the wonders of botany. She even began a course of physiology, but it chanced one day that next to the room at University College where she was studying, she heard the screams of a wretched dog who was being vivisected, and when told what it meant she burst into tears, realising her own helplessness to rescue the victim, and rushing out of the class-room in an agony of grief and indignation, never resumed her scientific studies, or went near the place again.

She turned to history, and was fortunate enough to hear Dr Creighton, now Bishop of London, at Cambridge. She delighted in Green's Short History, which had not nearly enough dates and battles to suit Norah. But what delighted Irene were the character sketches of Elizabeth, Mary Queen of Scots, Sir Thomas More, and the admirable narrative which laid bare the motives which swayed the popular and religious movements, the story of the Great Charter, the History of Puritanism, the reaction at the Restoration, the graphic touches which made William of Normandy, Henry II, Cecil Lord Burleigh, and Cromwell, as it were, step out of the dingy, moth-eaten, historical tapestries and become living presences once more.

Irene was an eager listener when clever men, statesmen, and politicians talked. She was not at all at sea. She had read John Stuart Mill's essay on 'Liberty' and his 'Representative Government,' and often surprised her friends by the clearness and penetration of her remarks upon questions affecting the pressure of taxation upon certain classes and the difficulties of political representation, so thoroughly had she imbibed the principle that all just taxation should be willing taxation, and that all free government should be, as Mazzini used to put it, government of the people, by the people, for the people.

But Irene was never a blue stocking. Her learning sat gracefully upon her; she wore it lightly, as she wore a rose in her hair, and she handled it as deftly as she used her racket at lawn tennis. Her own acquirements enabled her to get the most out of all the circles into which she entered, and she possessed the rare and sympathetic gift of imparting knowledge without making people feel their own ignorance.

Shall I look speculatively into Irene's future, as I made bold to sketch Norah's? She will not be in a hurry to marry, or eager to make a number of men propose whom she does not intend to accept. With a most kind and tender tact, the tact of a good woman, she will prevent them from proposing, and save them the pain and humiliation of a refusal. But Irene will marry in due time, and she will marry the man that suits her. Oddly enough, he will not be very intellectual, but he will adore her, and have a noble physique, and a generous and pure heart. She will not be the first girl he has been in love with, but the first girl he has ever been enough in love with to propose to. She will have her park, and her carriage and horses, and her little house in Mayfair. Her husband will be more a country gentleman than a club man, but he will be in Parliament and her drawing-room will be political, with an infusion of literary and artistic folk of the better sort, with very little of the neurotic and *fin-de-siècle* egotism and imposture about them.

For about five or six years after her marriage, Irene, who has two angelic little girls like herself and a brave romping boy with a strong likeness to her husband, will seem so absorbed by her children as to have forgotten her learning ; but her well-ordered mind will show itself in the admirable arrangement of her house, the fidelity of her servants, and the charming tact with which she manages her company and is able to draw out the varied qualities of all sorts and conditions of men and women. Her husband worships the ground she treads on ; but instead of domineering over him, she never forgets his position and prerogatives as head of the family, whilst she often allows him to shine by her light without his knowing it—perhaps without knowing it herself. For systematic study, which she loves, she naturally has not now so much time ; but as the girls grow up, all her old tendencies revive, and she lives her sunny past over again in their fresh young lives, directing their lessons, ordering their games and sports, and even firing the boy with noble ambitions which make him almost as great a success in the class-room as in the cricket-field.

Irene never loses her interest in the literature of the day. The great and at first overpowering grief of her life—the death of her husband about the time she is forty—she is slow to subdue her sorrow. She never marries again. The boy goes off a-soldiering in a crack regiment, the girls grow up charming women, but neither of them quite equal to their mother.

Before Irene is fifty she is a grandmother. She lives much more in the country than in town. She was never strictly philanthropic, but she now devises reading-rooms and clubs for working men, is the confidential adviser of the local parson, and is reverenced by her poorer neighbours as a person of infinite resource and inexhaustible kindness; nor is she ever tired of taking pains with everything and everybody.

Irene even once tries to get up a Shakespearean club for reading, but not even she can overcome the stolid indifference of the local gentry and their families to the cause of culture pure and simple. An exercise which does not lead to husbands, or benefit crops and live stock, has nothing to do with riding, hunting, flirting or even dining, of what use could such a thing be to the country folk of Bramble Foxley? So Irene accepts the situation, and contents herself by entertaining from time to time celebrated authors from London, and the M.P.'s whom her husband had known, who brought other younger M.P.'s, who married her girls.

So Irene, full of peace and good activities, according to her name, grows gracefully old, and her lovely hair becomes quite white and silvery; and wherever she goes people smile and feel happier.

Of all her learning nothing remains but a charming guide to the Art Galleries of Europe, dedicated to girls, and an equally well-written and admirably selected series of historical characters, each representing a distinct type of greatness or goodness.

But Irene's culture will have left its mark upon thousands of lives, and given a tone and a lift to countless households ; and whenever the time comes—and may it be far distant !—when a motto is sought for her tablet, I think I would have inscribed these favourite words of hers, which one of her daughters painted on a panel in her mother's bedroom : 'The heart of her that hath understanding seeketh knowledge, and a word spoken in season how good it is.'

Mannish
Girls

MANNISH
GIRLS

'WELL, my dear, I'm sorry to hear you want to shoot, and shoot pheasants, too. I should have thought that if you had once looked on at a battue— Of course, I know pheasants have to be eaten and killed, so have sheep ; but—'

'Stop,' says Clarisse, looking rather indignant.

But before I allow her to speak I should like to explain a little about Clarisse. She is a rosy-cheeked, high-spirited girl of eighteen, with a passion for gymnastics and golf, and she has a sort of hey-fellow-well-met, swashbuckler way with the men, which makes her a jolly companion for a picnic or an Alpine climb. She can pull a good oar, too, and boasts of being able to walk most men off their legs ; but that is a boisterous exaggeration, as she found out to her cost, when she laid herself up for a month, trying to tire out Charley Sparks, the champion

G

amateur light weight of Little Scuffleton-cum-Pancakes.

As she was boasting one day about her pedestrian feats with Charley, I said a little maliciously, 'Perhaps you forget that, after about eight miles, Charley looked back and saw you sitting on a stile, and supposing you meant to play him some prank, turned back and found —oh, well, you stuffed your pocket-handkerchief quickly out of sight, but it was quite clear you had been crying. It was very ignominious, but you know you had to go home in a baker's cart, which, as your mother said, by "a thankful blessing," happened to be passing, and Charley was so frightened that, although he had knocked you up, he ran six miles back by a short cut across the fields, and was found ready at the Warren, your father's house at Little S-cum-P, and lifted you out like a feather, although you are certainly a very well-developed, buxom girl.'

'Don't, don't!' cries Clarisse, quite angry. 'I've often walked as far and as fast as Charley, but that day I—I—'

'It does not in the least matter, my dear; but why do you want to walk as far and as fast as Charley?'

'Why, indeed! for the same reason that I want to shoot and play cricket. I don't see why the men should boast and brag that we poor weak women can't do this and that, as if we were a pack of invalids, forsooth, and the lords of creation alone were to walk abroad, and leave us cooped up in nurseries, kitchens, or eternally in bed.'

'But shooting, my dear!—delight in a practice which, however lawful, inflicts so much pain, and even prolonged torture, on the helpless feathered tribe! A woman's inclination is naturally on the side of pity, and the sight of—'

'Of course I don't take pleasure in the sufferings of the creatures, any more than I care for the fright and the death of the fox, except in so far as it adds excitement to the scrimmage. Then pheasant shooting is so clean, you know ; one doesn't *see* any blood. The birds are hit, and always pursued and quickly destroyed by the keepers.'

'Not always, Clarisse.'

'Well, anyhow, it's more amusing to go out a tramp in the woods and pop about amongst the birds, and do one's share with the men, than to loll about the house, sit over the fire with a novel, stroll out with a pack of children, or listen to the twaddle about babies and servants and complaints, and the curate. I'm sure the airs the men give themselves when they come back to lunch, boasting of the number of " heads " that fell to their guns—it is most wearing ! One may as well be in the running and do one's share, " Unfeminine," do you say ? I hate all that silly cant about women, and what they may and may not do. A few years ago it was " unfeminine " to play the violin, or even run about after you were twelve, or play lawn tennis, and only quite lately it has become lawful to bike.'

'Clarisse, you mix things up together. Of course, there is a certain margin allowed for fashion, and a discount for prejudice ; but a very little reflection and common sense, and, I may add, even some attention to the despised views of men, will enable a girl of intelligence and sensibility to distinguish between what is " feminine " and " unfeminine." Of course, a very pretty and clever woman will contrive to do even " unfeminine " things in a feminine way, just as a woman without tact or feeling will do feminine things in an unfeminine way. I saw Miriam Milford, at a meeting of her father's tenantry, in his enforced and sudden absence, preside in the chair at dinner over a very mixed company, and propose all the healths, and drink them too, with such a grace and bonhomie that the farmers when she rose to leave them, stood up on their chairs and cheered her till she was out of hearing. And Miriam is only nineteen, and supposed to be rather a shy girl. Yes, Clarisse, and I've seen your Cousin Louie bring in a cup of beef-tea to her convalescent mother, slamming the door with a back kick, and flopping down the food, with a "Here's the Bovril. Do you want anything else?" for all the world as if she was flinging a bone to a dog—and, of course, she trod on the cat as she went out. Now, nursing the sick is a very feminine occupation, no doubt, but it can be done in different ways.

'But to return to the question, What are becoming and unbecoming pursuits, and the reasons why?

'Do I object to cricket, for instance? Personally, I do not care to see a graceful girl straddling behind a wicket, with her nose above the bails, her body doubled-up like a frog's, and her hands clapped on her knees for support; nor do I think that a young lady's hands and arms were intended to swing a weighty club, and "swipe,"

as the boys say, at cricket balls. That young
ladies should have to caper about a field and
fall into hasty and often unbecoming attitudes,
and even tumble down whilst fielding, in the
presence of thousands of spectators, does not
" smile to me," as the French say, either. But
what chiefly prevents a male spectator from
enjoying the female cricket game is the fear
that a girl may be hit and injured fatally by
blows which man receives with comparative
impunity. The æsthetics of cricket may be
matters of taste, but the physics of cricket balls
are fixed quantities.'

'And lawn tennis ? '

'Why, excellent ! It has everything to recommend it—graceful exercise, skill, charming
attitudes, curves of beauty, and (a pleasing
and by no means a superfluous consideration)
the employment and enjoyment of both sexes.'

'And football ? '

'Detestable for girls ! '

'And biking ! '

'That depends. Nothing can be more grot-
esque than to see girls ape the grasshopper style
of the highroad " scorcher." The knickerbocker
Parisian male style of dress has been so debased
by caricatures in more than doubtful taste and

suggestive compromises, that I never wish to meet any knickerbocker girl in whom I am interested on a bike. Floppy and voluminous or carelessly worn skirts are also objectionable; but a tightly-fitting bodice and short, spare, tailor-made skirt, an upright but easy gait, a graceful seat, and a good knee and ankle action, not too high, and you have at once a combination of ease, celerity, and charm, which no male bicyclists can rival or approach. On the other hand, Clarisse, the manners of ladies on the road are apt to become horsey and brusque. These female Ariels on wheels as they scud by, with their detestable little bark or an impertinent jingle when close on some unwary pedestrian, do not always smack of refinement, or "that repose which stamps the caste," etc. The temptation to fling a gibe or a rebuke at some-one who cannot retaliate before Ariel is out of sight seems irresistible. "Now there, do you want to be run over?" "You don't know your right side, old man." "Stupid woman, can't you get out of the way?" I am sorry to say, Clarisse, I have heard such things from quite well-dressed women on the road. They did not seem aware that pedestrians might have some rights, and that they were the interlopers.'

'What do I think of the rubbish talked about girls injuring themselves by riding bikes?'

'Why, I think the unwholesome biking all comes from this chronic mania, which, I confess, seems to me to have seized upon you, Clarisse— the passion for aping and even outbidding men. Is it not enough for women to bike? Why must they bike like men, or as much as men? A man may do on a bike with impunity what a woman can't or ought not to do. A man can often overtire himself without serious harm, not so always a woman. A man can "scorch uphill," and half the women who injure themselves with biking do so from trying to scorch uphill—the strain of the uphill action is disastrous to the woman; but the man goes up before her, she is not going to be outdone, and up she goes after him, concealing her agonies or exhaustion, and the damage is done. The real secret of bicycling for women is that it carries their weight for them. Many women cannot stand or walk much; but once their weight is lifted, their hips, which are the strongest part—stronger in proportion than a man's—bear well the strain, and enable them to take the most exhilarating and healthy exercise.

'I daresay, my dear Clarisse, you would not

care for me to give you my opinion about golf
fishing, riding, driving, bow-and-arrow shooting
(far preferable and more graceful for ladies, by
the way, than rifle practice) ; but let me urge
upon you, my dear young lady, not to coarsen
yourself by aping the men, and thinking that
you score points by unsexing kinds of sport,
manly buttons, coats, boots, shirts, hats, and
above all, manly *slang*. Men laugh with these
sort of girls, and at them—they do to romp and
ride, and boat and climb with—but they don't
marry them, unless they are bullied or forced
into it. Men like girls who respect themselves.
Your funny, horsey, or odd girl is apt to give
herself away. You, my dear Clarisse, are not
yet too far gone on the wrong tack. You went
abroad to be finished at a French school. You
were a strong, healthy girl of sixteen, brought up
with rather boisterous brothers, who found your
petticoats excellent for the " long-stop," and made
use of you to climb trees and obtain nests, and
apples in orchards they were afraid to enter.
You were also handy at exercising the pony and
taking out the dogs. You could outrun all the
boys till you were twelve, and out-swim them,
too, at the seaside long after that; and you have
always pulled a good stroke—you were very

popular in the boat, because you did not care to steer. But at school Madame de-les-Graces, the lady superior, was shocked at your propensities to pelt the girls with pillows in the dormitory, and make hay of the bedclothes on summer mornings. Running and jumping also seemed to that good but French-bound lady scandalous ; and the dancing master was so shocked when you offered to show him how you could do the high kick, that he declared that if the *épouvantable* Miss Anglaise remained in the class, he must tender his '*demission*.' Poor Clarisse ! There was no harm in you, my dear, only your high spirits ran away with you ; but finding no sympathy at the Couvent du Parc, you decided that you had come amongst duffers who knew no better, and so you settled down and curbed your little ways, and then everyone saw what a nice, good-natured, warm-hearted girl you really were. And, indeed, you were much improved by ' Le Couvent,' and you quite won over Madame de-les-Graces, who kissed you and cried when you left. The girls all brought you flowers, and some of them had bits of your hair—which, of course, they stole, for you hated that sort of nonsense. And I am told even Alphonse, the shoeblack, looked tragic when "*la belle Miss*

Anglaise, avec les yeux si noirs et la bouche vermeille, et les beaux cheveux par bleu!" dropped two francs into his hand as he pursued her on board the steamer with her parasol and a *bonbonnière* she had left behind.

'Well, my dear girl, when you came back, the reaction was too strong. Your animal spirits suppressed, and very properly so, for two disciplinary but happy years, have now broken out, and you are two years older. In your own way you like the men, and you think a good deal about them, but not in the way of marriage, but as companions rather than lovers though you enjoy playing the tyrant, as all women do. But, Clarisse, you are on a false tack; and when those tomboy spirits of yours calm down, as you get on in the twenties, you will find that you have cultivated habits, mannerisms, and created impressions unfavourable to your happiness, and even prejudicial to your character, and all because you have set yourself to ape, rival, and imitate the men—very amusing at first, no doubt, so it seemed, but wrong, my dear, fundamentally wrong.

'I know some men are half women, and some women are half men; both are thus defective as ideal men and women. But you are not really unwomanly or half a man. You are warm-hearted, affectionate, and very true, and men's society supplies a real want in your nature. You are simply passing through a preposterous phase, founded on an entirely false estimate of your own nature and capacities. The heady talk of that strong-minded Miss Squails, who is so red, ugly, scraggy, and aggressive, but who somehow imposes her opinions on young girls, has muddled your judgment; but you will come all right when you have grasped a few fundamental points not in Miss Squails' catechism. Men and women are not equal, as Miss Squails would have you believe, in the sense of being identical in quality and capacity; they are equal by reason of different but equally valuable qualities and capacities. They may have much in common, intellect, feeling, intuition, and bodily functions; but the proportions are differently mixed and adjusted in the sexes. The sexes dominate each other by their differences and complimentary qualities, not their likenesses and equalities; and when a woman wears the breeches she is, or ought to be, as offensive to man, as a man disguised in petticoats is, or ought to be, offensive to a woman. You may retain all your wealth of spirits, your rich animal nature, your warm heart,

your sympathy with man and his pursuits; these
will help you to judge him fairly, and fit you to
offer and receive a wealth of love and sympathy
which a hypersensitive, neurotic, and less robust
woman in mind and body would be quite power-
less to yield. But the sooner you renounce
the "old chappie" and "tip us wink" style, the
better. The bravado of a cigar in the billiard-
room only lowers you in the eyes of those who
induce you to smoke it ; and the free use of
knickerbockers, rifles, cricket balls, and manly
coats, collars, ties, and waistcoats, rob you of
your womanhood without making you man, or
in the least adorable in the eyes of men, women,
or children.'

Poor Clarisse was getting extremely restless
as my homily proceeded. She was also looking
rather flushed and angry; but she showed no
signs of a hasty departure, and when I paused
she looked me straight in the face, her great
dark eyes flashing with something like un-
accustomed moisture—she was not one of the
weeping sort. I did not shrink from her gaze.
Suddenly the anger died out of her face, and she
put out her hand. I held it for a moment quite
impersonally, just as one holds the handle of
a drag when undetermined which way to push

it ; then I felt her firm plump hand and nervous fingers tighten on mine. I thought I had never seen her looking so handsome, and there was a rare touch of softness in her quite serious and self-contained oval face, and the slightest tremor in her lower lip, which steadied immediately. Yes, certainly Clarisse was a strong character.

'Thanks,' she said quite simply and frankly, as she loosed her grip. At that moment her favourite collie dog came bounding in by the open window from the lawn ; she turned quickly to caress him.

'Come along, Pompey ; we'll go for a long walk. I won't ask you to come with us,' she said ; 'I want to think !' and she ran out on to the lawn, as lithe as a child of ten, in full pursuit of Pompey.

I think two years passed and I hardly saw Clarisse. When I last heard of her, she had been for a whole year training as a nurse at the hospital. I understood that she was just engaged to the head doctor there—a young man of rising talent, who had already been summoned in consultation by Royalty, and even offered knighthood, but had declined it. Clarisse, they all said at home, was so changed, but changed for the better. It seems she had quite lost her taste for all those horsey and mannish things that were fast spoiling her ; but, added her mother, 'I hated the idea of her taking up hospital work, at first.'

'Ah, my dear lady,' I could not help saying, and to this day I don't know how the words came into my head, '*Counsel in the heart of woman is like deep water, but a woman of understanding will draw it out*' (Prov. xx. 5).

Engaged
Girls

ENGAGED
GIRLS

YES, Jessie, there were several young fellows
very glad to walk about the deck with you when
you went to America ; the *White Star* steamer
is well adapted to what censorious people might
call flirting. But, of course, there is flirting and
flirting. The term is susceptible of every shade
of meaning ; from the married woman or the
widow who keeps any number of men 'on'
—none of whom she will ever marry, or ever
intends to marry—to the fresh young girl just
out of the nursery, who has just discovered
that men like pretty eyes and dimpled cheeks,
and is brimming over with the fun of receiving
so much attention from young, middle-aged, and
old men. 'Oh,' says Jessie, who is just sixteen,
'Arthur is such a *nice boy;* but he has no conversation, and doesn't amuse me half as much as
smart Captain Checkham, who has been round

the world, and tells such lots of funny stories ;
and then he is *so* polite, and I don't call Arthur's
"manners " any manners at all.'

And so, when tea-time comes on board your
floating *White Star* palace, and Arthur—who
found you very useful as a long-stop two years
ago, and has spent a good bit of pocket-money
on you between then and now—sidles up to your
table, he finds Captain Checkham already seated
by you, showing you the jumping beans, and
rattling away about cannibals and alligators,
until of you, my poor Arthur—a freshman in his
first term—it may well be said, "'e dun know
where 'e are ! ' And you, malicious little Jessie,
well remembering how Arthur used to order
you about in the cricket-field and patronise you
at children's parties not so long ago, are quite
tickled at Arthur's discomfiture. And handsome
Checkham looks into your eyes, and quite by
chance touches your rosy-tipped fingers whilst
showing you the beans. He shows you those
beans over and over again ; you don't seem to
mind how often he explains the mystery of the
maggot inside, which wriggles when it feels the
warmth of his hand ; then you try yours, and
he puts his own brown manly paw gently on
your little plump white hand, just to show you

how ; and Arthur scowls, and goes off to another table ; and you laugh, and feel quite grown-up. Ah, Jessie, Jessie! this is the beginning of it all, my dear. Checkham has amused himself with scores of girls as pretty as you, and forgotten all about them ; but Arthur will never forget you. It is pleasant to trifle when the roses are blooming and the birds are singing in the springtime ; but a heart of gold and an honest hand are not found every day. But somehow girls will run after the Checkhams of this world, and the honest Arthurs go to the wall.

Three years go by. You, Jessie, are one of those girls who are bound to marry young. Oddly enough, Checkham has been hit this time. He meets you a year afterwards, in London. He has lost money—you, poor child, have got some ; he proposes — your silly little heart leaps to your mouth.

Oh, that conservatory, that easy-chair, the intoxicating scent of those heavy big lilies, and those fairy lights! Could you not notice anything wild about his eyes? Oh yes ! you thought it was love. No, it was want of sleep and—and—wine—but not want of wine, the results of too much ; but he only smelt of cigarettes, 'all men do,' you said. That was nothing ; he taught

you how to smoke one—it wasn't half bad. So,
Jessie, as he was not a bit shy, and seemed
very determined—poor little fluttering bird—
you lay very still and very close to his—let us
say waistcoat, and listened to the honeyed words;
and when you held your breath, and it came—
the proposal—you cried, and laughed, and said,
'Oh, Captain Checkham!' 'Say Jack,' he
whispered; and his hot breath was close to your
cheek and made your head swim, and you said,
'*Jack!*'—and your fate was sealed.

Jessie, you were only nineteen. Jack's family
was a good one; but he had made ducks and
drakes of his money. His uncle, who was fond
of him, had paid his debts—that is, the debts he
owned to, for such men never tell *all* their
debts—but he only paid them on condition that
Jack married and *settled down*; and you, poor
little thing, were the victim. Well, Jessie, long
before you married Jack—and you married him
within the year, when you were just twenty—you
had misgivings about him.

It was not very nice of him, when you had
only been engaged a fortnight, to ask so many
questions about your aunt's money and who
she was going to leave it to. Then that day
when you were driving in the park, and you

saw Jack talking to some one driving a smart pair
of cobs with a parasol-whip—she was a good
deal older than you ; in fact no longer very
young—Jack might have told you her name ;
not that it mattered, but still—

Then one day you got a very odd letter,
directed to you in Jack's handwriting, and
certainly the letter was in Jack's writing too,
and it began, 'Dearest, don't think,' etc. etc. ;
but you saw at once it was not meant for you,
for it referred to some supper party at which
you had not been present, and to someone
named Fanny, whom you did not know. You
kept the letter, of course, and showed it to Jack;
and he laughed and said it was all right, and
made a wonderfully full and elaborate explanation about a practical joke he had had with a
man, and a wager, and I know not what, and you
tried to swallow it all, and persuaded yourself
that it was quite simple, and— Only you were
not *quite* satisfied, and when you pressed Jack
further he got cross, almost sulky. So the
matter dropped.

Then you found that he had not told quite the
truth about why he never came to see you that
day when he promised to take you out, and
you sat all the afternoon with your bonnet on,

waiting; and that story about the mare going
lame was not in fact at all true, because he was
seen riding her in company with—with— And
you burst out crying, and he got angry, and in
fact he was downright unkind, and left you very
rudely, and did not come back for four days—
and you were to be married in a month !

And 'then you got an anonymous letter in a
female hand, and then—well, there were tears
and explanations—and you were to be married
the week after ! And oh—Jessie *before* you
married him you felt he did not half love you
and although you loved him dearly he had
done and said things to you—such things—you
could not quite respect him.

Meanwhile Arthur went to China, and is not
married yet ; and you had not been married one
year when you wrote to dear old (she was only
twenty-two) Margaret Browne, your bosom
friend. 'Oh, Margy, I wish I had never known
Jack—and I had married Arthur !' Now, the
moral of all this, my dear girl-reader, whoever
you are, is—don't take a leap in the dark.
Don't accept *anyone* in a hurry. It is the most
important step of your life ; look before you
leap. You are at a picnic ; you get lost—with
someone else. The mossy bank with the prim-

roses, and the blue sky just seen through the budding branches of early spring, the stillness of the summer noontide and the sudden seclusion, the sort of dream-life which comes over you both, and robs you of your judgment, power of comparison, and general sanity—beware! And oh! whatever follies you may drift into at such a moment, Heaven forfend that you should accept a proposal of marriage then and there!

Flushed with the dance, straying out into the soft moonlight air on the lawn, then into the plantation path with the over-arching trees above you, then sinking on a rustic bench just to listen for a moment to the long-drawn-out sweetness of the nightingale, whilst an arm steals round your waist—my dear Adelaide, do keep your presence of mind. Of course Augustus may be just the right person for you, but not then and not there should be the decisive moment. Not to accept is quite a different thing from refusing. Give him hope, let him even believe in your half-consent; but wait and see how it all looks the next morning. There is no fear of losing him if he is worth having; you may be sure that he will call for an answer.

But how can girls know, before they have been engaged a little while, whether there is any real chance of permanent happiness? An engagement is a sort of probation ; and whilst no one can feel more strongly than I do about breaking off engagements capriciously, I say deliberately that if a girl, after she is engaged, finds out such things about her lover as Jessie found out about Jack Checkham—things which make it impossible for her, even in the light and heat of his glowing suit, ever to respect him— she is justified in stopping short in time. If even on further acquaintance there is radical disparity of tastes, and opposition, even physical opposition, of temperaments—in short, a discord of affinities—why should two young people run into life-long misery with their eyes open ?

And yet this is what many parents and guardians are tempted to advise, and even urge young girls to do, because it is 'so bad for a girl to break off her engagement ! '

Is it not, then, worse for a girl to run headlong into a life that is worse than death, and make peradventure the misery of two lives—not counting the lamentable disorder and unhappiness of children demoralised by the spectacle of a house divided against itself?

The girl who has the presence of mind to say ' No ' in time, after she has either conscientiously, deliberately, or hastily said 'Yes,' has my respect ; for I believe that in so doing she is consulting her own and her lover's best interests, as well as the welfare and morality of the social circle in which she moves.

When a girl becomes engaged I sometimes notice that her mind seems unsettled and unhinged. She relaxes her attention to household or educational duties ; she is impatient with Sissy over her music lesson ; cannot answer Granny's tiresome questions affably ; finds it a burden to do her mother's commissions ; and forgets to answer letters — except when the answers are addressed to Charles.

Sometimes her engagement acts differently upon her. It so quickens and heightens all her life that she is sweeter to everyone. Her nature seems suddenly deepened and enriched ; she hugs the little children, and kisses her pet cat, or dog, or rabbit ; cares lovingly for the suffering, the sick poor ; is all smiles for the village children who meet her and bob curtseys, all tears and tenderness for those in distress, and an angel of comfort to those suffering from disappointment—especially disappointment in love.

Of course a good deal will depend upon temperament, but something ought to depend upon principle.

Because you are engaged, Lucille, you need not be petulant or negligent of household duties ; neither need you make yourself ridiculous by an exuberance of sentiment. But what you ought really to do is to prepare yourself in every way you can during those engaged months for the great change of life which is approaching. You must not suppose that marriage is a state in which all restraint can be safely thrown to the winds ; where at last you are going to have your own way, and do what you like. Marriage calls for more restraint, more discretion, more sacrifice than single life. Never did you need to lay to heart those words, ' Watch and pray that ye enter not into temptation,' more than in the first few months or years of married life.

Then, Lucille, before you marry you should at once take stock of your husband's family— how you may ingratiate yourself with his mother, please his father, and work in with his sisters. Don't be like those foolish girls who begin by mak- ing enemies of their husband's sisters. *They* may have just cause to feel a little jealous of *you*, for perhaps you are monopolising and are about to carry off their favourite brother ; but *you* are little

likely to have much cause to be jealous of *them*
—you have an irresistible pull over them because
you possess Charles ; and if they are sensible
girls (and girls are fairly sensible and sympathetic
about other people's love affairs, providing these
don't interfere with their own) Charles' sisters
will get to like you if you try to like them, and
don't domineer and give yourself airs ; and by-
and - bye they will be such nice aunts, and so
good to your children, as the new interests grow
up. And remember what an advantage it will be
all round for you and your family to be accept-
able to Charles and his family ; and how many
things—opportunities, interests, and pleasures—
you will all miss if discord is sown, and you are
not on speaking terms, and people have to take
sides, fight, and ' fool around ' generally, instead
of cultivating forbearance and goodwill betimes,
and trying to live happily together.

But, my dear Lucille, the engaged months
will do much to determine these family relations
for better or for worse. You see that Mimé is
jealous of you—it will nearly break her heart
to lose Charles. Now you've got to *win Mimé*.
If you don't, she will be spiteful ; she will set
Adèle and George, and perhaps her mother,
against you. Poor Mimé ! perhaps you can't

help it ; you can't see anything nice or good in
the girl who takes away your favourite brother.
But Mimé is to be won, and is worth winning,
Lucille, early— do not lose a day. Work at Mimé
—her warm but wounded heart will make your
task easier than you think ; make her feel she
will always be welcome ; and Mimé will change,
perhaps quite suddenly. Appeal to what is
generous, not to what is mean and selfish in her;
and because she loves Charles, she will end by
loving you, when you take her to your arms like
a sister ; and if you make Charles happy she will
learn to love you for that too. Only Mimé must
not be shut out ; the separation must be softened
for her by your love and sympathy. All this
requires tact, restraint, thought, unselfishness.
Oh, believe me, Lucille, the engaged months as
well as the married years are seasons for cultivating self-sacrifice, seasons for thoughtful discipline, patience, and a large, wise charity and
forbearance.

And, my dear child, if you only knew a little
cooking, and paid some attention to accounts,
and got your mother to show you how to house-
keep, and mastered the price of necessaries at
shops, and the duties of servants, it would save
you many mistakes and vexations, which some-

times ruffle the peace of those critical months which immediately follow the honeymoon.

The engaged girl will shortly go forth to fill a new sphere. Upon her depends the general tone of her husband's home; she is not only there for his personal satisfaction and pleasure, but for the general direction of an establishment, which long after her beauty has faded will be stamped with an undying grace or disgrace. Character, method, thought, moral qualities, my dear, outlast personal beauty, and are wont even to shine through them; these, too, are what make the happiness of a home. Does not even the sad preacher of Ecclesiasticus say of a wife, 'Nothing is so much worth as a mind well instructed'; and again, 'A faithful woman is a double grace, and her continent mind cannot be valued;' and yet once more, 'As the sun when it ariseth in the high heaven, so is the beauty of a good wife in the ordering of her house?'

Brides

BRIDES

THE moment has at last come—you are a bride. You surrender

> The pond with all its lilies for the leap
> Into the unknown deep.

You now begin to find out the sort of man you have married. The honeymoon, next to the month in which you were born, and next to the month in which you have got to die, is perhaps the most important month of your life.

How many brides know how to spend their honeymoon well?—and how many bridegrooms? The extreme seclusion and mutual self-absorption, supposed to be the correct thing for people just married, is a great mistake. You have got to spend years in each other's society, why not economise a little? Economy of money is not the only thing needful. There is such a thing as economy of strength, of feeling, of enjoyment, and of opportunity. Things grow by that they feed on *up to a point*, and then sets in hypertrophy and deterioration from over supply. I remember at a great hotel in Paris, watching a very nice young couple, evidently on their nuptial trip, in the reading-room after dinner. They were looking already dreadfully bored. I suppose they had been cooped up together all day, and any one who came across them would shun them as newly-married people who must be left to each other. This may have been going on for a week or more for aught know. I at once seemed to read their history. They had explored Paris—churches, Champs Elysée, the Magazins, shops (which Edward did try to like)—but perhaps were never out of each other's sight all day. Once, indeed, Edward had said after dinner, 'Look here, Aggie; I want just to go out and have a smoke on the Boulevard. You know, love, you are tired out; had you not better go to bed early?' Well, Aggie, you are at once filled with vague alarms. Edward apparently likes his pipe better than his bride; you don't say so, but you look it. But Edward doesn't mean that at all. Edward feels after days of sweet communion, and such a lovely time with you, and all that, that—that if he could only be alone, quietly alone in the fresh air with his

pipe, and think—think about his happiness, and
his new plans, and his life—his life past, as well
as present and future! Indeed, he positively
craves for solitude; he can't exactly explain
what he feels, but after dinner to go into that
reading-room, when his wife is too tired to go
out with him, and dawdle about respectably for
half-an-hour, and pretend to look at the *Journal
Illustré*, *Galignani*, or *Punch*, because it seems
stupid or dull to go upstairs so soon! Why
should not Edward go out for a stroll, and come
in fresh, and find Aggie comfortably asleep?
The poor child, if she would only admit it, wants
that quiet sleep more than anything else.

This constant companionship, though so precious, is so strange, and well—really a little
overstrain to the mind; and suppose Edward
feels the same in his way, what harm is
done by an hour—two hours—of interrupted
connubial felicity? No harm of any kind is
done, or intended to be done; good is done.
Then why that pout, and that little frown of
pain, and the almost irritable and certainly
irritating 'Don't be long.' There is perhaps
nothing a man hates more than a woman's—
even a dear woman's—'Don't be long.' It makes
him feel tied by the leg like a bird with a string,

and some one to pull it at the other end. Now, a man will be a woman's willing captive, but the sense of her curtailing his freedom, instead of allowing him voluntarily to surrender it himself, that he cannot endure. Neither does a man like to account for every moment of his time; not necessarily because he has anything to be ashamed of, or that he can't account for it satisfactorily, but because he has often nothing to tell, which is of course unsatisfactory; and then if his bride, as so many raw brides are, is intolerably exacting and inquisitive whenever he goes out, he feels that an account will be expected, and he must recollect all he does—which is a great bore—in order to have a coherent narrative ready. For young married people there is nothing like timely and judicious solitude, and letting each other alone, when it comes naturally, and may be needed—literally needed—by both. There are subtle and only half-understood conditions of exhausted personal magnetism, which only rest and comparative isolation, or cessation of close contact, and generally changed magnetic conditions, such as we gain from association with others, can restore.

Have you not heard people say, ' I can't stand So and So for *very long?* ' or an invalid will tell

you, ' So and So exhausts and depletes me, seems
to drain my life, whilst others refresh me. I
love to have them sit by my side, the feel of
their hand is delicious and full of strength ; but
curiously enough, after a time, I am not sensitive
to it.'

The fact is, we are all of us more or less like
a Leyden jar ; we absorb and discharge magnetic
shocks, contact draws out our nerve-life, and it
must be replenished before we can have any
more to give ; and with some people, and at
some times, our expenditure and receptivity of
subtle nerve-currents which are after all the
vehicles of thought, affection, and all other
emotion, is much greater than at others. All
which things nine out of ten brides and bridegrooms—although such things are most pertinent
to them—are quite ignorant of, and so they drift
into ill-humour and ennui, and those other
psychological climates which breed disaffection
and discord—ay, sometimes before the honeymoon is well over. Believe me, I don't want
you to be a blue-stocking in the sense of a
mannish New Woman. Whatever you study,
you should remember that first of all your glory
is to be a woman, and to wear your knowledge
and wisdom gracefully ; but a little of the

common-sense side of physiology, metaphysics,
and psychology would do a bride no harm ; and
the engaged girl would probably have a happier
honeymoon for knowing more often than she
does what she is about in the honeymoon, and
what are the inalienable and inexorable conditions which will make and keep two souls and
bodies happy and at ease in each other's close
company. If I were writing for the young man,
I should, of course, have a lot of good advice to
give him about his bride and himself. He will
require to have forbearance ; he must learn to
postpone himself, to deny himself, to be gentle,
chivalrous, thoughtful, indulgent, but withal
firm too when needful. But it is with you,
little girl-wife, not him, that I have now to do.

Let me caution you, then, not to overdraw
the bank of love. You may fancy that the
instant you are married you will have it all
your own way, and if Edward is a gentleman,
so you will, *at first*. But that bridal power of
yours is a perilous gift ; it is a charm you can
easily trifle with, and which is apt to lose
its efficacy before you are aware of it, and your
awakening may be rude.

Edward smokes. Your mother does not like
smoke, no more do you. ' When Edward is

married,' you say, ' Edward won't smoke ; he will do as I choose.' So when Edward says, on the second day of your wedding tour, in the railway carriage, ' You don't mind my having a cigarette if I open the window, do you, darling ? ' you put on a little frown, and you say in a wounded way, ' You know I hate tobacco.' And Edward winces a little ; but as he is a good fellow, and loves you dearly, he says, ' All right, my pet ; I don't care, if you don't like it.' But he has made his first sacrifice. He feels you have made him *pay* for the pleasure of your company, and the bloom of the transaction is off. But the next day, conversation having run a little dry, Edward takes out his pipe. ' I say, Aggie, you just let me have a whiff or two ; I can sit over here, you know, by the window, and it won't hurt you ; ' but *you*, silly girl, exclaim, ' I hate your horrid nasty pipe ! ' and although he has lighted up, you go over to his side, and you take it out of his mouth, and then there is a little struggle, half play of course, but you spoil all by saying, ' Shan't smoke whilst I'm here, anyhow.' And as Edward is a *very* good fellow, he gives a little forced laugh, takes you round the waist, kisses you, and says, ' Oh, very well, dear ; I did not know you minded so

K

much as all that,' and so he gulps down his growing annoyance, and it passes off.

But the next day you steal his tobacco-pouch, and the day after perhaps you take his pipe away, and even break it—a short clay. 'Oh, I say, Aggie, I was colouring that clay—it took me six months, and was getting on splendidly; you need not have done that.' Well, it is wonderful what a young fellow will put up with not to quarrel with his girl-wife.

After all, women don't know so much about men's lives before they marry, although they think they do. As a rule, men know a great deal more about girls' lives, or think they do! And so a man will be patient and gradual and indulgent with his bride *up to a point*. But, after all, they have got to live together and share alike, and sooner or later, if Aggie steals his pouch, throws his best birdseye out of the window, and breaks his favourite pipe, Edward will know the reason why. That's man's way. So I say to Aggie, 'Be careful, my dear; your overdraft on the bank of love will be honoured once and twice and thrice, but one day your cheque will come back upon you with "No assets," or "Not sufficient," written across it, and you may have some difficulty in restoring the lost balance.'

Some people will tell you that you need not know anything about married life until it comes, and then it will all come naturally. No doubt it will. So will smallpox, and typhoid and scarlet fever, and if you recover you will probably have learned some useful lessons about bad air and bad water and drains and dust-heaps, which will enable you to avoid another attack of these pestilent maladies. Now, a little thought, knowledge, and previous instruction would save many a girl from those pestilential quarrels, those exhausting, depleting, lethiferous discords, those malarious and infected '*psychological climates*.' (I thank Mr A. J. Balfour for the words) into which brides are hurried because they have not been taught to avoid them in early married life.

And Aggie, if you have been a spoilt child, in the habit of crying for the moon and having it at once handed down to you, it is impossible, to conceive any more critical time for you than the first six months of your married life.

You have put it off till now, but your moral education has to begin at last and begin at once.

Kneel down, my dear child, whoever you are, on the eve of your marriage, and ere you surrender your maiden name and your girlhood, kneel down beside your little narrow white bed for the last time, and pray that God will give you the understanding heart, so that in quietness and confidence you may possess your own soul, and go to the man who will make you his own, 'all bathed in angel instincts,' ready to be taught the will of the Heavenly Father and the conduct of the perfect life.

> To give or keep, to live and learn to be
> All that not harms distinctive womanhood,
> Nor lose the childlike in the larger mind.
> Till at the last you set yourself to move
> Like perfect music unto noble words.

THE END

J. Miller & Son, Printers, Edinburgh.

A Selected List

of

Books

published by

Mr James Bowden
London

American Agency

M. F. Mansfield
22 East Sixteenth Street
New York

SECOND EDITION.

Crown 8vo, cloth gilt, $1.25.

The 'Paradise' Coal Boat

By Cutcliffe Hyne,

Author of "The Recipe for Diamonds," &c.

" In Mr Cutcliffe Hyne our great Anglo-Indian romancer (Rudyard Kipling) seems to have found a worthy comrade. . . . Grim and powerful tales. . . . Alike from a literary and political point of view Mr Cutcliffe Hyne has, in his latest volume, deserved well of the commonwealth."—*The Echo.*

" Mr Hyne knows the sea, and the seamy side of sea life. He also knows the West Coast of Africa, and whether we are voyaging with him in a tramp steamer between London and Shields, or off the Lagos Coast, we feel that we are somehow in the proper atmosphere. Constructively his stories are always excellent."—*The Scotsman.*

" Mr Hyne knows the secret of free and boisterous life on land and sea ; he can spin a smuggler's yarn, or tell a tale of lynching with the best man going."—*Morning Leader.*

"In his tales of the sea, in his pictures of life on reckless traders, in his types of dare-devil seamen, Mr Hyne is only equalled by Rudyard Kipling."—*Pall Mall Gazette.*

" They are not only capital light reading, but they give us an insight into phases of life well outside the hackneyed range of fiction."—*The Sun.*

" Notably distinct in their force and virility from the general run of short stories."—*Daily Mail.*

" One of the best of recent volumes of stories."—*To-Day.*

" We can heartily commend the volume. . . . Highly entertaining and thoroughly realistic sketches of certain phases of colonial and seafaring life."—*Bradford Telegraph.*

" All the tales are interesting, and some of them, in their way, are very nearly as good as good can be. . . . Your attention is held, your pulses are stirred, and you are heartily sorry when you get to the end of the book. . . . We doubt if stories like 'The "Paradise" Coal Boat' and 'The Salvage Hunters' could possibly be bettered."—*Daily Chronicle.*

SECOND EDITION.

Crown 8vo, cloth gilt, $1.25.

Methodist Idylls

By Harry Lindsay.

" Worthy of any writer who has yet set himself to depict Methodist life. . . . A very helpful and right religious book."—*Methodist Times.*

" A book which in its lovely prose chapters gives an insight into the true romance, the April sunshine, of Methodist life. . . . We hope that the volume may find its way into every Methodist home."—*Methodist Recorder.*

" A most admirable attempt to throw into permanent form some portraits of the old and vanishing Methodists. . . . As a study in Methodism, Mr Lindsay's work can be cordially and heartily commended."—*The Sun.*

" Mr Lindsay's Methodist stories are told with great power and sympathy. The book is certainly a very striking success in its own way."—*The Academy.*

" These village sketches will be read with pleasure by young and old. . . . There is a genuine appreciation of the religious life of a village, and a tender handling of some of the homely comedies and tragedies."—*London Quarterly Review.*

" A most admirable attempt to throw into permanent form some portraits of the old and vanishing Methodist. . . . Truly some of these men were the 'salt of the earth.' . . . As a study in Methodism Mr Lindsay's book can be cordially and heartily commended."—*The Sun.*

" It is no exaggeration to say that 'Methodist Idylls' is one of the most refreshing and wholesome books which we have lately had offered to us, or that its author's powers are great, and likely to be still greater."—*Leeds Mercury.*

" Mr Lindsay has done Methodism an invaluable service by embodying its forms and beliefs in these lovable personalities. The book deepens in power as we read on, and holds us with a firm grip to the end. . . . A feast of good things."—*Christian World.*

" Extremely interesting stories . . . admirably told."—*The Scotsman.*

" Cannot fail to delight Methodist readers of all sections, but more particularly the members of the older Wesleyan Church. . . . All the way through the religious teaching is delightful."—*Christian Age.*

A BOOK OF YACHTING STORIES
FOR HOLIDAY READING.

Crown 8vo, cloth, price $1.00.

The Paper Boat

By "Palinurus."

OPINIONS OF THE PRESS.

" Lively tales of yachting adventure. . . . 'The Paper Boat' will be a pleasant companion on any cruise, and we wish her a prosperous voyage on her own account as well."—*Glasgow Herald.*

" Bright and amusing. . . . There is some charming description in the book, which is in every respect eminently readable, making no heavy demands on the reader, and keeping him in good humour."—*The Sportsman.*

" Brightly written stories of the sea. . . . The stories have a brightness and freshness which cannot fail to give pleasure."—*Manchester Courier.*

" We unreservedly recommend this book to any one on holiday as a sure tonic against business worries and city soot. It has the same effect as a whip of salt spray on the face of a jaded worker."—*N. B. Daily Mail.*

" The author writes with strength and picturesqueness on a subject of which he is evidently a master, and one cannot read his stories without a thrill of the excitement that is one of the greatest charms of yachting."—*Dundee Advertiser.*

" A charming volume in all respects. . . . A more delightful story, or better told, than 'The Voyage of the Florette' there could not be. We envy those who have not read it. The book is full of life and go."—*Sheffield Telegraph.*

" As bright and breezy as can be wished. . . . One of the best volumes of light short stories offered to the public for a long time past."—*Lloyd's Newspaper.*

Litanies of Life

By Kathleen Watson.

Mr T. P. O'CONNOR, M.P., in *The Weekly Sun*
("A Book of the Week")

" Fancy a woman . . . so gifted, sitting down with the resolve to crush into a few words the infinite tale of all the whole race of her sex can suffer, and you have an idea of what this remarkable book is like. . . . As wonderful an epitome of a world of sorrow as I have ever read."

" A work of great charm, over which one likes to linger, and dream, and think. . . . The words flow with that tuneful felicity which belongs more to poetry than to prose."—*Liverpool Post.*

" The five short, poignant stories which make up this excellent little book, are remarkable for distinction of style, and interesting by reason of the writer's observation of life and character, and the originality of her reflections. . . . Miss Watson can tell a story in a way to cut the reader to the heart. . . . The reader of sensibility will find a chastened pleasure in every one of them."—*The Morning.*

" So real is this first sketch, so human, so sensitively delicate, so successful in its curious mingling of boldness and tenderness, that the reader necessarily imagines it to be autobiographical, believing that only out of actual sorrow could be distilled so true a record of passion and of regret."—*The Daily Mail.*

" Written in most admirable prose, this collection of five beautiful, though sad stories, will appeal to all lovers of good literature. . . . It adds to its worth as a clever book the additional charm of being a good one."—*Lloyd's Newspaper.*

Crown 8vo, cloth elegant, gilt top, $1.00.

The Widow Woman

A CORNISH TALE.

By Charles Lee.

OPINIONS OF THE PRESS.

" Such a delightfully natural love story is this that even staid old people who have not read one for a score of years will admit that it is quite unromantic enough to be sensible. . . . We close the book with a feeling of gratitude to the author who has supplied us with such a delightful study."—*Manchester Courier.*

" A delightful little work. . . . Mr Lee knows these fisher folk by heart, and has the ability to draw them to the life in a few bright strokes of drollery. . . . The character sketching is admirable, the scenes and situations are most vividly brought out, and the pervading humour is of a genuine stamp."—*Sheffield Independent.*

" An entertaining story. . . . A clever, humorous and thoroughly enjoyable book."—*Scotsman.*

" A fascinating book. . . . From beginning to end it is delightfully fresh and vigorous; the vignettes of Cornish life and character are quaint and humorous ; and the snatches of unsophisticated philosophy, not without a dash of subtlety, are as amusing as they are original. . . . Nothing so deliciously witty as John Trehill's courtship has been written of late, and another story from the author's pen will be awaited with the keenest pleasure and interest."—*Dundee Advertiser.*

" The story, simple and homely in its nature, is told with a humour and abandon that makes the book most delightful reading."—*Glasgow Daily Mail.*

" The book is one to read, having the blessed quality of making you chuckle : the best of qualities in literature, one is inclined to say, in these tired days."—*Black and White.*

STORIES OF LOWER LONDON.

Crown 8vo, cloth gilt, $1.25.

East End Idylls

By A. St John Adcock.

"This is a remarkable book. It is a collection of short stories on East End life, but they are told with that real realism of observation of which Mr Morrison has set the fashion. The setting is real, the slang is real, the manners and customs seem to have been drawn from life."—*The Daily News.*

"It does not need any actual experience of East End life to tell the reader of these 'East End Idylls' that they are the work of a master-hand. . . . The little idylls are all exquisitely done -exquisitely, we say, because there is no other word which will do full justice to the performance."—*The Sun.*

"Very vivid sketches of the East End as it is to-day. In the intimacy they display with life in the slums, and in the terseness and force of their style, they boldly challenge comparison with 'Tales of Mean Streets,' nor do they lose by the comparison. Mr Adcock's themes are less gloomy and hopeless than Mr Morrison's. Amid all the misery he loves to recount deeds of unselfish devotion and simple heroism ; nor do I believe that he is less true to life because his realism is less grim."—*The Pall Mall Gazette.*

"Distinctly a book worth reading. There is heroism here, and knowledge — true insight, in fact—and sympathy." — *The Leeds Mercury.*

"A series of touching and delightful sketches. Much has been written of the East End, but rarely with more charm or sympathy than by Mr Adcock."—*The Star.*

"Mr Adcock possesses a graphic pen, and has sketched the loves and hates, the joys and the sorrows of the dwellers in London's mighty East in a series of short, vigorous stories that make up a very delightful volume."—*Lloyd's Newspaper.*

www.ingramcontent.com/pod-product-compliance
Lightning Source LLC
Chambersburg PA
CBHW030903050726
47500CB00009B/1006